Daniel Jackson

Alonzo and Melissa;

The unfeeling father. An American Tale

Daniel Jackson

Alonzo and Melissa;
The unfeeling father. An American Tale

ISBN/EAN: 9783337024727

Printed in Europe, USA, Canada, Australia, Japan

Cover: Foto ©Andreas Hilbeck / pixelio.de

More available books at **www.hansebooks.com**

ALONZO AND MELISSA;

OR,

THE UNFEELING FATHER.

𝔄𝔫 𝔄𝔪𝔢𝔯𝔦𝔠𝔞𝔫 𝔗𝔞𝔩𝔢.

"In every varied posture, place, and hour,
How widowed every thought of every joy!"
YOUNG.

BY DANIEL JACKSON, JR.

PHILADELPHIA:
CLAXTON, REMSEN & HAFFELFINGER,
624, 626 & 628 MARKET STREET.
1879.

PREFACE.

WHETHER the story of Alonzo and Melissa will generally please, the writer knows not; if, however, he is not mistaken, it is not unfriendly to religion and to virtue.— One thing was aimed to be shown, that a firm reliance on Providence, however the affections might be at war with its dispensations, is the only source of consolation in the gloomy hours of affliction; and that generally such dependence, though crossed by difficulties and perplexities, will be crowned with victory at last.

It is also believed that the story contains no indecorous stimulants; nor is it filled with unmeaning and inexplicated incidents sounding upon the sense, but imperceptible to the understanding. When anxieties have been excited by involved and doubtful events, they are afterwards elucidated by the consequences.

The writer believes that generally he has copied nature. In the ardent prospects raised in youthful bosoms, the almost consummation of their wishes, their sudden and unexpected disappointment, the sorrows of separation, the joyous and unlooked for meeting—in the poignant feelings of Alonzo, when, at the grave of Melissa, he poured the feelings of his anguished soul over her miniature by the "moon's pale ray;"—— when Melissa, sinking on her knees before her father, was received to his bosom as a beloved daughter risen from the dead.

If these scenes are not imperfectly drawn, they will not fail to interest the refined sensibilities of the reader.

ALONZO AND MELISSA.

A TALE.

IN the time of the late revolution, two young gentlemen of Connecticut, who had formed an indissoluble friendship, graduated at Yale College in New-Haven : their names were Edgar and Alonzo. Edgar was the son of a respectable farmer. Alonzo's father was an eminent merchant. Edgar was designed for the desk, Alonzo for the bar; but as they were allowed some vacant time after their graduation before they entered upon their professional studies, they improved this interim in mutual, friendly visits, mingling with select parties in the amusements of the day, and in travelling through some parts of the United States.

Edgar had a sister who, for some time, had resided with her cousin at New-Lonlon. She was now about to return, and it was designed that Edgar should go and attend her home. Previous to the day on which he was to set out, he was unfortunately thrown from his horse, which so much injured him as to prevent his prose-

cuting his intended journey : he therefore
invited Alonzo to supply his place; which
invitation he readily accepted, and on the
day appointed set out for New-London,
where he arrived, delivered his introductory
letters to Edgar's cousin, and was received
with the most friendly politeness.

Melissa, the sister of Edgar, was about six-
teen years of age.   She was not what is esteemed a striking beauty, but her appearance
was pleasingly interesting.   Her figure was
elegant; her aspect was attempered with a
pensive mildness, which in her cheerful
moments would light up into sprightliness
and vivacity.   Though on first impression,
her countenance was marked by a sweet and
thoughtful serenity, yet she eminently possessed the power to

" Call round her laughing eyes, in playful turns,
The glance that lightens, and the smile that burns."

Her mind was adorned with those delicate
graces which are the first ornaments of female excellence.   Her manners were graceful without affectation, and her taste had been
properly directed by a suitable education.

Alonzo was about twenty-one years old ;
he had been esteemed an excellent student.
His appearance was manly, open and free.
His eye indicated a nobleness of soul; although his aspect was tinged with melancholy, yet he was naturally cheerful.   His
disposition was of the romantic cast;

For far beyond the pride and pomp of power,
He lov'd the realms of nature to explore ;
With lingering gaze Edinian spring survey'd ;
Morn's fairy splendours ; night's gay curtained shade,
The high hoar cliff, the grove's benighting gloom,
The wild rose, widowed o'er the mouldering tomb ;
The heaven embosom'd sun ; the rainbow's dye,
Where lucid forms disport to fancy's eye ;
The vernal flower, mild autumn's purpling glow,
The summer's thunder and the winter's snow."

It was evening when Alonzo arrived at the house of Edgar's cousin. Melissa was at a ball which had been given on a matrimonial occasion in the town. Her cousin waited on Alonzo to the ball, and introduced him to Melissa, who received him with politeness. She was dressed in white, embroidered and spangled with rich silver lace, a silk girdle, enwrought and tasseled with gold, surrounded her waist; her hair was unadorned except by a wreath of artificial flowers, studded by a single diamond.

After the ball closed, they returned to the house of Edgar's cousin. Melissa's partner at the ball was the son of a gentleman of independent fortune in New-London. He was a gay young man, aged about twenty-five. His address was easy, his manners rather voluptuous than refined; confident, but not ungraceful. He led the ton in fashionable circles; gave taste its zest, and was quite a favorite with the ladies generally. His name was Beauman.

Edgar's cousin proposed to detain Alonzo and Melissa a few days, during which time

they passed in visiting select friends and socia.
parties. Beauman was an assiduous attend-
ant upon Melissa. He came one afternoon
to invite her to ride out ;—she was indisposed and excused herself. At evening she
proposed walking out with her cousin and
his lady; but they were prevented from
attending her by unexpected company.
Alonzo offered to accompany her. It was
one of those beautiful evenings in the month
of June, when nature in those parts of A-
merica is arrayed in her richest dress. They
left the town and walked through fields
adjoining the harbour.—The moon shone
in full lustre, her white beams trembling
upon the glassy main, where skiffs and sails
of various descriptions were passing and
repassing. The shores of Long-Island and
the other islands in the harbour, appeared
dimly to float among the waves. The air
was adorned with the fragrance of surrounding flowers ; the sound of instrumental music
wafted from the town, rendered sweeter by
distance, while the whippoorwill's sprightly
song echoed along the adjacent groves. Far
in the eastern horizon hung a pile of brazen clouds, which had passed from the north,
over which, the crinkling red lightning momentarily darted, and at times, long peals of
thunder were faintly heard. They walked
to a point of the beach, where stood a large

rock whose base was washed by every tide. On this rock they seated themselves, and enjoyed a while the splendours of the scene—the drapery of nature. "To this place, said Melissa, have I taken many a solitary walk, on such an evening as this, and seated on this rock, have I experienced more pleasing sensations than I ever received in the most splendid ball-room." The idea impressed the mind of Alonzo; it was congenial with the feeling of his soul.

They returned at a late hour, and the next day set out for home. Beauman handed Melissa into the carriage, and he, with Edgar's cousin and his lady, attended them on their first day's journey. They put up at night at the house of an acquaintance in Branford. The next morning they parted · Melissa's cousin, his lady and Beauman, returned to New-London; Alonzo and Melissa pursued their journey, and at evening arrived at her father's house, which was in the westerly part of the state.

Melissa was received with joyful tenderness by her friends. Edgar soon recovered from his fall, and cheerfulness again assumed its most pleasing aspect in the family.—Edgar's father was a plain Connecticut farmer. He was rich, and his riches had been acquired by his diligent attention to business. He had loaned money, and taken

mortgages on lands and houses for securi-
ties; and as payment frequently failed, he
often had opportunities of purchasing the
involved premises at his own price.   He
well knew the worth of a shilling, and how
to apply it to its best use; and in casting
interest, he was sure never to lose a far-
thing.   He had no other children except
Edgar and Melissa, on whom he doated.—
Destitute of literature himself, he had provided the means of obtaining it for his son,
and as he was a rigid presbyterian, he considered that Edgar could no where figure so
well, or gain more eminence, than in the
sacred desk.

The time now arrived when Edgar and
Alonzo were to part.   The former repaired
to New-York, where he was to enter upon
his professional studies.   The latter entered in the office of an eminent attorney in
his native town, which was about twenty
miles distant from the village in which lived the family of Edgar and Melissa.   A-
lonzo was the frequent guest of this family;
for though Edgar was absent, there was still
a charm which attracted him hither. If he
had admired the manly virtues of the brother, could he fail to adore the sublimer
graces of the sister? If all the sympathies
of the most ardent friendship had been drawn
forth towards the former, must not the most

tender passions of the soul be attracted by
the milder and more refined excellencies of
the other?

Beauman had become the suitor of Melissa; but the distance of residence rendered it inconvenient to visit her often. He
came regularly once in two or three months;
of course Alonzo and he sometimes met.
Beauman had made no serious pretensions,
but his particularity indicated something
more than fashionable politeness.

His manners, his independent situation,
his family, entitled him to respect. "It is
not probable therefore that he will be objec-
tionable to Melissa's friends or to Melissa
herself," said Alonzo, with an involuntary
sigh.

But as Beauman's visits to Melissa became
more frequent, an increasing anxiety took
place in Alonzo's bosom. He wished her
to remain single; the idea of losing her by
marriage, gave him inexpressible regret.
What substitute could supply the happy
hours he had passed in her company? What
charm could wing the lingering moments
when she was gone? In the recess of his
studies, he could, in a few hours, be at the
seat of her father: there his cares were
dissipated, and the troubles of life, real or
imaginary, on light pinions, fleeted away.—
How different would be the scene when

debarred from the unreserved friendship and conversation of Melissa; And unreserved it could not be, were she not exclusively mistress of herself.   But was there not something of a more refined texture than friendship in his predilection for the company of Melissa? If so, why not avow it? His prospects, his family, and of course his pretensions might not be inferior to those of Beauman.   But perhaps Beauman was preferred.   His opportunities had been greater; he had formed an acquaintance with her.   Distance proved no barrier to his addresses.   His visits became more and more frequent.   Was it not then highly probable that he had secured her affections? Thus reasoned Alonzo, but the reasoning tended not to allay the tempest which was gathering in his bosom.   He ordered his horse, and was in a short time at the seat of Melissa's father.

It was summer, and towards evening when he arrived.   Melissa was sitting by the window when he entered the hall. She arose and received him with a smile.   "I have just been thinking of an evening's walk, said she, but had no one to attend me, and you have come just in time to perform that office. I will order tea immediately, while you rest from the fatigues of your journey."

When tea was served up, a servant entered the room with a letter which he had found in the yard.   Melissa received it.— " 'Tis a letter, said she, which I sent by Beauman, to a lady in New-London, and the careless man has lost it."   Turning to Alonzo, " I forgot to tell you that your friend Beauman has been with us a few days ; he left us this morning."

" My friend !" replied Alonzo, hastily.

"Is he not your friend?" enquired Melissa.

" I beg pardon, madam," answered he, " my mind was absent."

" He requested us to present his respects to his friend Alonzo," said she.   Alonzo bowed and turned the conversation.

They walked out and took a winding path which led along pleasant fields by a gliding stream, through a little grove and up a sloping eminence, which commanded an extensive prospect of the surrounding country ; Long Island, and the sound between that and the main land, and the opening thereof to the distant ocean.

A soft and silent shower had descended a thousand transitory gems trembled upon the foliage glittering the western ray.—A bright rainbow sat upon a southern cloud ; the light gales whispered among the branches, agitated the young harvest to billowy motion, or waved the tops of the distant

2

deep green forest with majestic grandeur. Flocks, herds, and cottages were scattered over the variegated landscape.

Hills piled on hills, receding, faded from the pursuing eye, mingling with the blue mist which hovered around the extreme verge of the horizon. "This is a most delightful scene," said Melissa.

"It is indeed, replied Alonzo; can New-London boast so charming a prospect?"

Melissa. No—yes; indeed I can hardly say. You know, Alonzo, how I am charmed with the rock at the point of the beach.

Alonzo. You told me of the happy hours you had passed at that place. Perhaps the company which attended you there, gave the scenery its highest embellishment.

Melissa. I know not how it happened; but you are the only person who ever attended me there.

Alonzo. That is a little surprising.

Mel. Why surprising?

Al. Where was Beauman?

Mel. Perhaps he was not fond of soli tude. Besides he was not always my Beau man.

Al. Sometimes.

Mel. Yes, sometimes.

Al. And now always.

Mel. Not this evening.

Al. He formerly

Mel. Well.

Al. And will soon claim the exclusive privilege so to do.

Mel. That does not follow of course.

Al. Of course, if his intentions are sincere, and the wishes of another should accord therewith.

Mel. Who am I to understand by another?

Al. Melissa. [A pause ensued.]

Mel. See that ship, Alonzo, coming up the sound; how she ploughs through the white foam, while the breezes flutter among the sails, varying with the beams of the sun.

Al. Yes, it is almost down.

Mel. What is almost down?

Al. The sun. Was not you speaking of the sun, madam?

Mel. Your mind is absent, Alonzo; I was speaking of yonder ship.

Al. I beg pardon, madam. O yes—the ship—it—it bounds with rapid motion over the waves.

A pause ensued. They walked leisurely around the hill, and moved toward home. The sun sunk behind the western hills.—Twilight arose in the east, and floated along the air. Darkness began to hover around the woodlands and vallies. The beauties of the landscape slowly receded. "This reminds me of our walk at New-London,"

said Melissa. "Do you remember it?" enquired Alonzo. "Certainly I do," she replied, " I shall never forget the sweet pensive scenery of my favourite rock." "Nor
I neither," said Alonzo with a deep drawn
sigh.

The next day Alonzo returned to his
studies; but, different from his former visits
to Melissa, instead of exhilarating his spirits,
this had tended to depress them. He doubted whether Melissa was not already engaged to Beauman. His hopes would persuade him that this was not the case; but
his fears declared otherwise.

It was some time before Alonzo renewed
his visit. In the interim he received a letter
from a friend in the neighbourhood of Melissa's father; an extract from which follows:

" We are soon to have a wedding here;
you are acquainted with the parties—Melissa D—— and Beauman. Such at least
is our opinion from appearances, as Beauman is now here more than half his time.—
You will undoubtedly be a guest. We had
expected that you would have put in your
claims, from your particular attention to the
lady. She is a fine girl, Alonzo."

" I shall never be a guest at Melissa's
wedding," said Alonzo, as he hastily paced
the room; "but I must once again see her
before that event takes place, when i lose

her forever." The next day he repaired
to her father's. He enquired for Melissa,
she was gone with a party to the shores of
the sound, attended by Beauman. At evening they returned. Beauman and Alonzo
addressed each other with much seeming
cordiality. "You have deceived us, Alonzo, said Melissa. We concluded you had
forgotten the road to this place."

" Was not that a hasty conclusion ?" replied Alonzo. " I think not, she answered,
if your long absence should be construed
into neglect. But we will hear your ex
cuse, said she, smiling, by and by, and perhaps pardon you." He thanked her for
her condescension.

The next morning Beauman set out for
New-London. Alonzo observed that he
took a tender leave of Melissa, telling her,
in a low voice, that he should have the happiness of seeing her again within two or
three weeks. After he was gone, as Melissa and Alonzo were sitting in a room a-
lone, "Well, said she, am I to hear your
excuses ?"

Alonzo. For what, madam ?

Mel. For neglecting your friends.

Alonzo. I hope it is not so considered,
madam.

Mel. Seriously, then, why have you
2 *   A

stayed away so long? Has this place ro charms in the absence of my brother?

Al. Would my presence have added to your felicities, Melissa?

Mel. You never came an unwelcome visiter here.

Al. Perhaps I might be sometimes intrusive.

Mel. What times?

Al. When Beauman is your guest.

Mel. I have supposed you were on friendly terms.

Al. We are.

Mel. Why then intrusive?

Al. There are seasons when friendship must yield its pretensions to a superior claim.

Mel. Perhaps I do not rightly comprehend the force of that remark.

Al. Was Beauman here, my position might be demonstrated.

Mel. I think I understand you.

Al. And acknowledge my observation to be just?

Mel. (hesitating.) Yes—I believe I must.

Al. And appropriate?

Melissa was silent

Al You hesitate, Melissa.

was still silent.

Will you, Melissa, answer me one

Mel. (confused.) If it be a proper one you are entitled to candour.

Al. Are you engaged to Beauman?

Mel. (blushing.) He has asked me the same question concerning you.

Al. Do you prefer him to any other?

Mel. (deeply blushing, her eyes cast upon the floor.) He has made the same enquiry respecting you

Al. Has he asked your father's permission to address you?

Mel. That I have not suffered him yet to do.

Al. Yet!

Mel. I assure you I have not.

Al. (taking her hand with anxiety.) Melissa, I beg you will deal candidly. I am entitled to no claims, but you know what my heart would ask. I will bow to your decision. Beauman or Alonzo must relinquish their pretensions. We cannot share the blessing.

Mel. (her cheeks suffused with a varying glow, her lips pale, her voice tremulous, her eyes still cast down.) My parents have informed me that it is improper to receive the particular addresses of more than one. I am conscious of my inadvertency, and that the reproof is just. One therefore must be dismissed. But—(she hesitated.)

A considerable pause ensued. At length

Alonzo arose—" I will not press you farther," said he ; " I know the delicacy of your feeling, I know your sincerity ; I will not therefore insist on you performing the painful task of deciding against me. Your conduct in every point of view has been discreet. I could have no just claims, or if I had, your heart must sanction them, or they would be unhallowed and unjustifiable. I shall ever pray for your felicity.—Our affections are not under our direction ; our happiness depends on our obedience to their mandates. Whatever, then, may be my sufferings, you are unblameable and irreproachable." He took his hat in extreme agitation, and prepared to take his leave.

Melissa had recovered in some degree from her embarrassment, and collected her scattered spirits. " Your conduct, Alonzo, said she, is generous and noble. Will you give yourself the trouble, and do me the honour to see me once more ?" " I will, said he, at any time you shall appoint."— "Four weeks then, she said, from this day, honour me with a visit, and you shall have my decision, and receive my final answer." " I will be punctual to the day," he replied, and bade her adieu.

Alonzo's hours now winged heavily away. His wonted cheerfulness fled ; he wooed the silent and solitary haunts of " musing, moping melancholy." He loved to wander through lonely fields, or along the verge of some lingering stream, "when dewy twilight rob'd the evening mild," or "to trace the forest glen, through which the moon darted her silvery intercepted ray."

He was fondly indulging a tender passion which preyed upon his peace, and deeply disturbed his repose. He looked anxiously to the hour when Melissa was to make her decision. He wished, yet dreaded the event. In that he foresaw, or thought he foresaw, a withering blight to his budding hopes, and a final consummation to his foreboding fears. He had pressed Melissa, perhaps too urgently, to a declaration.—Had her predilection been in his favour, would she have hesitated to avow it? Her parents had advised her to relinquish, and had permitted her to retain one suitor, nor had they attempted to influence or direct her choice. Was it not evident, then, from her confused hesitation and embarrassment, when solicited to discriminate upon the subject, that her ultimate decision would be in favour of Beauman?

While Alonzo's mind was thus agitated, he received a second letter from his friend in the neighbourhood of Melissa. He read the following clause therein with emotions more easily to be conceived than expressed :

"Melissa's wedding day is appointed.   I need not tell you that Beauman is to be the happy deity of the hymeneal sacrifice.   I had this from his own declaration.   He did not name the positive day, but it is certainly to be soon.   You will undoubtedly, however, have timely notice, as a guest.   We must pour a liberal libation upon the mystic altar, Alonzo, and twine the nuptial garland with wreaths of joy.   Beauman ought to devote a rich offering to so valuable a prize.   He has been here for a week, and departed for New-London yesterday, but is shortly to return."

"And why have I ever doubted this e-vent ? said Alonzo.   What infatuation hath thus led me on the pursuit of fantastic and unreal bliss ?   I have had, it is true, no posi-tive assurance that Melissa would favour my addresses.   But why did she ever receive them ?   Why did she enchantingly smile upon me ?   Why fascinate the tender powers of my soul by that winning mildness, and the favourable display of those complicated and superior attractions which she must have known were irresistible ?—Why did she not spurn me from her confidence, and plainly tell me that my attentions were untimely and improper ?   And now she would have me dance attendance to her decision in fa-vour of Beauman—Insulting ! Let Beauman

and she make, as they have formed, this
farcical decision; I absolutely will never
attend it.—But stop: I have engaged to see
her at an appointed time ; my honour is
therefore pledged for an interview; it must
take place.   I shall support it with becoming dignity, and I will convince Melissa and
Beauman that I am not the dupe of their
caprices.   But let me consider—What has
Melissa done to deserve censure or reproach?
Her brother was my early friend : she has
treated me as a friend to her brother.   She
was unconscious of the flame which her
charms had kindled in my bosom.—Her
evident embarrassment and confusion on receiving my declaration, witnessed her surprise and prior attachment.   What could
she do ? To save herself the pain of a direct
denial, she had appointed a day when her
refusal may come in a more delicate and
formal manner—and I must meet it."

At the appointed day, Alonzo proceeded
to the house of Melissa's father, where he
arrived late in the afternoon.   Melissa had
retired to a little summer house at the end
of the garden ; a servant conducted Alonzo
thither.   She was dressed in a flowing robe
of white muslin, embroidered with a deep
fringe lace.   Her hair hung loosely upon
her shoulders ; she was contemplating a
bouquet of flowers which she held in her

nand. Alonzo fancied she never appeared
so lovely. She arose to receive him. "We
have been expecting you some time, said
Melissa; we were anxious to inform you,
that we have just received a letter from my
brother, in which he desires us to present
you his most friendly respects, and complains
of your not writing to him lately so frequently as usual." Alonzo thanked her for
the information; said that business prevented him; he esteemed him as his most valuable friend, and would be more particular
in future.

"We have been thronged with company
for several days, said Melissa. Once a year
my father celebrates his birth day, when we
are honoured with so numerous a company
of uncles, aunts, cousins, nephews and nieces,
that were you present, you would suppose we
were connected with half the families in Connecticut. The last of this company took
their departure yesterday, and I have only
to regret, that I have for nearly a week, been
prevented from visiting my favourite hill, to
which you attended me when you was last
here. It is much improved since then: I
have had a little arbour built under the large
tree on its summit: you will have no objection to view it, Alonzo?" He assured
her he accepted the invitation with pleasure.

and towards evening they resorted to the place and seated themselves in the arbour.

It was the beginning of autumn, and a yellow hue was spread over the fading charms of nature. The withering forest began to shed its decaying foliage, which the light gales pursued along the russet fields. The low sun extended the lengthening shadows; curling smoke ascended from the surrounding cottages. A thick fog crept along the vallies; a gray mist hovered over the tops of the mountains. The glassy surface of the sound glittered to the sun's departing ray. The solemn herds lowed in monotonous symphony. The autumnal insects in sympathetic wafting, plaintively predicted their approaching fate. "The scene is changed since we last visited this place, said Melissa; the gay charms of summer are beginning to decay, and must soon yield their splendors to the rude despoiling hand of winter."

"That will be the case, said Alonzo, before I shall have the pleasure of your company here again."

Mel. That probably may be, though it is nearly two months yet to winter.

Al. Great changes may take place within that time.

Mel. Yes, changes must take place; but

3

nothing, I hope, to embitter present prospects.

Al. (peevishly.) As it respects yourself, I trust not, madam.

Mel. (tenderly.) And I sincerely hope
not, as it respects you, Alonzo.

Al. That wish, I believe, is vain.

Mel. Why so ominous a prediction?

Al. The premises, from which it is
drawn, are correct.

Mel. Your feelings accord with the season, Alonzo; you are melancholy   Shall
we return?

Al. I ask your pardon, madam; I know
I am unsociable. You speak of returning:
You know the occasion of my being here.

Mel. For the purpose of visiting your
friends, I presume.

Al. And no other?

She made no reply.

Al. You cannot have forgotten your own
appointment, and consequent engagement?

She made no answer.

Al. I know, Melissa, that you are inca-
pable of duplicity or evasion. I have promised, and now repeat the declaration, that
I will silently submit to your decision. This
you have engaged to make, and this is the
time you have appointed. The pains of present suspense can scarcely be surpassed by
the pangs of disappointment. On your part

you have nothing to fear. I trust you have candidly determined, and will decide explicitly.

Mel. (sighing.) I am placed in an exceedingly delicate situation.

Al. I know you are; but your own honour, your own peace, require that you should extricate yourself from the perplexing embarrassment.

Mel. I am sensible they do. It must—it shall be done.

Al. And the sooner it is done the better.

Mel. That I am convinced of. I now know that I have been inadvertently indiscreet. I have admitted the addresses of Beauman and yourself, without calculating or expecting the consequences. You have both treated me honourably, and with respect. You are both on equal grounds as to your character and standing in life. With Beauman I became first acquainted. As it relates to him, some new arrangements have taken place since you were here, which——

Al. (interrupting her, with emotion.) Of those arrangements I am acquainted.

Mel. (surprised.) By what means were you informed thereof?

Al. I received it from a friend in your neighbourhood.

A considerable pause ensued.

Al.   You see, Melissa, I am prepared for
the event.—She was silent.

Al. . I have mentioned before, that, whatever be your decision, no impropriety can
attach to you.   I might not, indeed, from
various circumstances, and from the information I possess, I perhaps should not, have
given you farther trouble on the occasion,
had it not been from your own direction
and appointment.   And I am now willing
to retire without further explanation, without giving you the pain of an express decision, if you think the measure expedient.
Your declaration can only be a matter of
form, the consequence of which I know,
and my proposition may save your feelings.

Mel.   No, Alonzo; my reputation depends on my adherence to my first determination; justice to yourself and to Beauman also demand it.   After what has passed, I should be considered as acting capri-
ciously and inconsistently, should I depart
from it.   Beauman will be here to-morrow,
and——

Al.   To-morrow, madam?

Mel.   He will be here to-morrow, and
you must consent to stay with us until that
time; the matter shall then be decided.

Al.   I—yes—it shall be as you say, madam.   Make your arrangements as you
please.

Evening had now spread her dusky mantle over the face of nature. The stars glistened in the sky. The breeze's rustling wing was in the tree. The "slitty sound" of the low marmuring brook, and the far off water-fall, were faintly heard. The twinkling fire-fly arose from the surrounding verdure and illuminated the air with a thousand transient gleams. The mingling discordance of curs and watch-dogs echoed in the distant village, from whence the frequent lights darted their palely lustre thro' the gloom. The solitary whippoorwills stationed themselves along the woody glens, the groves and rocky pastures, and sung a requiem to departed summer. ·A dark cloud was rising in the west, across whose gloomy front the vivid lightning bent its forky spires.

Alonzo and Melissa moved slowly to the village; she appeared enraptured with the melancholy splendours of the evening, but the other subject engaged the mental attention of Alonzo.

Beauman arrived the next day. He gave his hand to Alonzo with seeming warmth of friendship. If it was reciprocated, it must have been affected. There was no alteration in the manners and conversation of Melissa : her conversation, as usual, was sprightly and interesting. After dinner she retired, and her father requested Alonzo and Beauman to withdraw with him to a private room. After they were seated, the old gentlemen thus addressed them:

"I have called you here, gentlemen, to perform my duty as a parent to my daughter, and as a friend to you. You are both suitors to Melissa ; while your addresses were merely formal, they were innocent; but when they became serious they were dangerous. Your pretensions I consider equal, and between honourable pretenders, who are worthy of my daughter, I shall not attempt to influence her choice. That choice, however, can rest only on one: she has engaged to decide between you. I am come to make, in her name, this decision. The following are my terms :—No quarrel or difficulty shall arise between you, gentlemen, in consequence of her determination. Nothing shall go abroad respecting the affair; it shall be ended under my roof. As soon as I have pronounced her declaration, you shall both depart and absent my house for at least two weeks, as it would be improper for my daughter to see either of you at present: after that period I shall be happy to receive your visits."—Alonzo and Beauman pledged their honour to abide implicitly by these injunctions. Her father then observed—"This, gentlemen, is all I require. I have observed that I considered your pretensions equal: so has my daughter treated them. You have both made professions to her; she has appointed a time to answer you. That time has arrived, and I now inform you that she has decided in favour of—Alonzo."

The declaration of Melissa's father burst upon the mental powers of Beauman, like a sudden and tremendous clap of thunder on the deep and solemn silence of night. Unaccustomed to disappointment, he had calculated on success. His addresses to the ladies had ever been honourably received.

Melissa was the first whose charms were capable of rendering them sincere. He was not ignorant of Alonzo's attention to her: it gave him however but little uneasiness. He believed that his superior qualifications would eclipse the pretensions of his rival. He considered himself a connoisseur in character, especially in the character of the ladies. He conformed to their taste; he flattered their foibles, and obsequiously bowed to the minutia of female volatility. He considered himself skilled in the language of the heart; and he trusted that from his pre-eminent powers in the science of affection, he had only to see, to sue and to conquer. He had frankly offered his hand to Melissa, and pressed her for a decisive answer. This from time to time she suspended, and finally appointed a day to give him and Alonzo a determinate answer, though neither knew the arrangements made with the other.

Finding, however, the dilemma in which she was placed, she had previously consulted her parents. Her father had no objection to her choosing between two persons of equal claims to affluence and reputation; this choice she had made, and her father was considered the most proper person to pronounce it.

When Beauman had urged his suit to Melissa, he supposed that her hesitations, delays and suspensions, were only the effects of maiden diffidence and timidity. He had no suspicions of her ultimately rejecting it; and when she finally named the day of decision, he was confident she would decide in his favour. These sentiments he had communicated to the person who had written to Alonzo, intimating that Melissa had fixed a time which was to crown his happiest wishes.

He had listened therefore attentively to the words of Melissa's father, momentarily expecting to hear himself declared the favourite choice of the fair.

What then must have been his disappointment when the name of Alonzo was pronounced instead of his own! The highly finished scene of pleasure and future prosperity which his ardent imagination had depicted, had vanished in a moment. The rainbow glories which gilded his youthful horizon, had faded in an instant—the bright sun of his early hopes had set in mournful darkness. The summons of death would not have been more unexpected, or more shocking to his imagination.

Very different were the sensations which inspired the bosom of Alonzo. He had not even calculated on a decision in his own favour. He believed that Beauman would be the choice of Melissa. She had told him that the form of decision was necessary to save appearances: with this form he complied because she desired it, not because he expected the result would be in his favour. He had not therefore attended to the words of Melissa's father with that eagerness which favourable anticipations commonly produce. But when his name was mentioned; when he found he was the choice—the happy favourite of Melissa's affection, every tender passion of his soul became interested, and was suddenly aroused to the refinements of sensibility. Like an electric shock, it reanimated his whole frame, and vibrated every nerve of his heart. The glooms which hung about his mind were dissipated, and

B

the bright morning of joy broke in upon his soul.

Thus were the expectations of Alonzo and Beauman disappointed—how differently, the sequel has shown.

Melissa's father retired immediately after pronouncing the declaration; the two young gentlemen also soon after withdrew. Alonzo saw the tempest which tore the bosom of his rival, and he pitied him from his heart.

A fortnight passed, and Alonzo felt all that anxiety and impatience which a separation from a beloved object can produce. He framed a thousand excuses to visit Melissa, yet he feared a visit might be premature. He was, however, necessitated to make a journey to a distant part of the country, after which he resolved to see Melissa. He performed his business, and was returning. It was toward evening, and the day had been uncommonly sultry for the autumnal season. A rising shower blackened the western hemisphere; the dark vapour ascended in folding ridges, and the thunder rolled at a distance. Alonzo saw he should be overtaken. He discovered an elegant seat about one hundred yards distant from the road; thither he hastened to gain shelter from the approaching storm. The owner of the mansion met him at the door, politely invited him to alight and walk in, while a servant stood ready to take his horse. He was ushered into a large room neatly furnished, where the family and several young ladies were sitting. As Alonzo glanced his eyes hastily around the room, he thought he recognized a familiar countenance. A hurried succession of confused ideas for a moment crossed his recollection. In a moment he discovered that it was Melissa. By this unexpected meeting they were both completely embarrassed. Melissa, however, arose, and in rather a confused manner, introduced Alonzo, as the classmate of her brother, to the family of Mr. Simpson and the company.

The rain continued most part of the afternoon. Alonzo was invited, and consented to stay all night. A moon-light evening succeeded the shower, which invited the young people to walk in an adjoining garden. Melissa told Alonzo that Mr. Simpson was a distant relative of her father; his family consisted of his wife, two amiable daughters, not far from Melissa's age, and one son, named William, about seventeen years old. She had been invited there to pass a week, and expected to return within two days. And she added, smiling, " perhaps, Alonzo, we may have an opportunity once more to visit the bower on my prospect hill, before winter entirely destroys the remaining beauties of the summer." Alonzo felt all the force of the remark. He recollected the conversation when they were last at the place she mentioned; and he well remembered his feelings on that occasion.

"Great changes, indeed, he replied, have taken place since we were last there : that they are productive of unexpected and unexampled happiness to me, is due, Melissa, to you alone." Alonzo departed the next morning, appointing the next week to visit Melissa at her father's house.

Thus were the obstacles removed which presented a barrier to the united wishes of Alonzo and Melissa. They had not, it is true, been separated by wide seas, unfeeling parents, or the rigorous laws of war; but troubles, vexations, doubts and difficulties, had thus far attended them, which had now disappeared, and they calculated on no unpropitious event which might thwart their future union. All the time that Alonzo could spare from his studies was devoted to Melissa, and their parents began to calculate on joining their hands as soon as Alonzo's professional term of study was completed.

The troubles which gave rise to the disseveration of England from America had already commenced, which broke out the ensuing spring into actual hostilities, by the battle at Lexington, followed soon after by the battle at Bunker Hill. The panic and general bustle which took place in America on these events, is yet well remembered by many. They were not calculated to impress the mind of Melissa with the most pleasing sensations. She foresaw that the burden of the war must rest on the American youth, and she trembled in anticipation for the fate of Alonzo. He, with others, should the war continue, must take the field, in defence of his country. The effects of such a separation were dubious and gloomy. Alonzo and she frequently discoursed, and they agreed to form the mystic union previous to any wide separation.

One event tended to hasten this resolution. The attorney in whose office Alonzo was clerk, received a commission in the new raised American army, and marched to the lines near Boston. His business was therefore suspended, and Alonzo returned to the house of his father. He considered that he could not long remain a mere spectator of the contest, and that it might soon be his duty to take the field; he therefore concluded it best to hasten his marriage with Melissa. She consented to the proposition, and their parents made the necessary arrangements for the event. They had even fixed upon the place which was to be the

4

future residence of this happy couple. It
was a pleasantly situated village, surrounded by rugged elevations, which gave an air
of serenity and seclusion to the valley they
encircled.   On the south arose a spacious
hill, which was ascended by a gradual ac-
clivity ; its sides and summit interspersed
with orchards, arbours, and cultivated fields.
On the west, forests unevenly lifted their
rude heads, with here and there a solitary
field, newly cleared, and thinly scattered
with cottages.   To the cast, the eye extended over a soil, at one time swelling into
craggy elevations, and at another spreading
itself into vales of the most enchanting verdure.   To the north it extended over a vast
succession of mountains, wooded to their
summits, and throwing their shadows over
intervales of equal wilderness, till at length
it was arrested in its excursions by the blue
mists which hovered over mountains more
grand, majestic and lofty.*   A rivulet which
rushed from the hills, formed a little lake
on the borders of the village, which beauti-
fully reflected the cottages from its transpar-
ent bosom.   Amidst a cluster of locusts and
weeping willows, rose the spire of the church,
in the ungarnished decency of Sunday neat
ness.   Fields, gardens, meadows, and pas-

*Some who read this description will readily recognize the
village here described.

ι ͻ were spread around the valley, and on
the sides of the declivities, yielding in
their season the rich flowers, fruits and foliage of spring, summer and autumn. The
inhabitants of this modern Auvernum were
mostly farmers. They were mild, sociable,
moral and diligent. The produce of their
own flocks and fields gave them most of
their food and clothing. To dissipation
they were strangers, and the luxuries of
their tables were few.

Such was the place for the residence of
Alonzo and Melissa. They had visited the
spot, and were enraptured with its pensive,
romantic beauties. A site was marked out
whereon to erect their family mansion. It
was on a little eminence which sloped gradually to the lake, in the most pleasant part
of the village. " Here, said Alonzo one
day to Melissa, will we pass our days in all
that felicity of mind which the chequered
scenes of life admit. In the spring we will
rove among the flowers. In summer, we
will gather strawberries in yonder fields, or
whortleberries from the adjacent shrubbery.
The breezes of fragrant morning, and the
sighs of the evening gale, will be mingled
with the songs of the thousand various bird
which frequent the surrounding groves.
We will gather the bending fruits of autumn,
and we will listen to the hoarse voice of

winter, its whistling winds, its driving snow, and rattling hail, with delight."

The bright gems of joy glistened in the eyes of Melissa. With Alonzo she anticipated approaching happiness, and her bosom beat in rapturous unison.

Winter came on; it rapidly passed away. Spring advanced, and the marriage day was appointed.

The spring opened with the din of preparation throughout America for defensive war. It now was found that vigorous measures must be pursued to oppose the torrent which was preparing to overwhelm the colonies, which had now been dissevered from the British empire, by the declaration of independence. The continental army was now raising, and great numbers of American youth volunteered in the service of their country. A large army of reinforcements was soon expected from England to land on our shores, and " the confused noise of the warriors, and garments rolled in blood," were already anticipated.

Alonzo had received a commission in a regiment of militia, and was pressed by several young gentlemen of his acquaintance, who had entered the army, to join it also. He had an excuse. His father was a man in extensive business, was considerably past the prime of life, had a number of agents

and clerks under him, but began to grow
unable to attend to the various and bur-
thensome duties and demands of a mercantile life.

Alonzo was his only son; his assistance
therefore became necessary until, at least,
his father could bring his business to a close,
which he was now about to effect. Alonzo
stated these facts to his friends; told them
that on every occasion he should be ready
to fly to the post of danger when his country was invaded, and that as soon as his father's affairs should be settled, he would, if
necessary, willingly join the army.

The day now rapidly approached when
Alonzo was to make Melissa his own. Preparations for the hymeneal ceremony were
making, and invitations had already gone
abroad. Edgar, the brother of Melissa
had entered the army in the capacity of
chaplain. He was soon expected home,
where he intended to tarry until the consummation of the nuptials, before he set out
for the camp. Letters recently received
from him, informed that he expected to be
at his father's in three or four days.

About three weeks previous to the appointed marriage day, Alonzo and Melissa
one afternoon rode out to the village which
had been chosen for their future residence.
Their carriage stopped at the only inn in the

place, and from thence they walked around
this modern Vaucluse, charmed with the secluded beauties of its situation.   They passed a little time at the spot selected for their
habitation ; they projected the structure of
the buildings, planned the gardens, the artificial groves, the walks, the mead, the
fountains, and the green retreat of the summer house, and they already saw, in anticipation, the various domestic blessings and
felicities with which they were to be surrounded.

They took tea at the inn, and prepared to
return. It was at the latter end of the
month of May, and nature was adorned in
the bridal ornaments of spring ; the sun was
sunk behind the groves, which cast their
sombre shades over the valley, while the
retiring beams of day adorned the distant
eastern eminences with yellow lustre.

'The birds sung melodiously in the groves,
the air was freshened by light western breezes, bearing upon their wings all the entrancing odours of the season.   Around the
horizon, electric clouds raised their brazen
summits, based in the black vapour of approaching night.

They slowly ascended the hill south of
the town, where they paused a few moments to enjoy the splendours of the evening scene. This hill, which commanded a

prospect of all the surrounding country, the
distant sound, and the adjacent towns and
villages, presented to the eye, on a single
view, perhaps one of the most picturesque
draperies painted by nature. Alonzo attended Melissa to her father's, and the next
day returned home.

His father had been absent for three or
four days to one of the commercial seaports,
on business with some merchants with whom
he was connected in trade. He returned
the next day after Alonzo got home :—his
aspect and his conversation were marked
with an assumed and unmeaning cheerfulness. At supper he ate nothing, discoursed much, but in an unconnected and hurried manner, interrupted by long pauses, in
which he appeared to be buried in contemplation.

After supper, he asked Alonzo if it were
not possible that his marriage with Melissa
could be consummated within a few days.
Alonzo, startled at so unexpected a question, replied, that such a proposal would be
considered extraordinary, perhaps imprope.
besides, when Melissa had fixed the day
she mentioned that she had an uncle who
lived near Charleston, in South Carolina,
whose daughter was to pass the summer
with Melissa, and was expected to arrive before the appointed day. It would he said,

be a delicate point for him to requ *. t* her to
anticipate the nuptials, unless he could give
some cogent reasons for so doing; and at
present he was not apprised that any such
existed.   His father, after a few moments
hesitation, answered, "I have reasons,
which, when told"—here he stopped, suddenly arose, hastily walked the room in
much vissible agony of mind, and then retired to his chamber.

Alonzo and his mother were much amaz-
ed at so strange a proceeding.   They could
form no conjecture of its cause or its consequence.   Alonzo passed a sleepless night.
His father's slumbers were interrupted. He
would frequently start up in the bed, then
sink in restless sleep, with incoherent mut-
terings, and plaintive moans.   In the morning, when he appeared at breakfast, his
countenance wore the marks of dejection
and anguish.

He scarcely spoke a word, and after the
table was removed, he ordered all to withdraw except his wife and Alonzo; when,
with emotions that spoke the painful feelings of his bosom, he thus addressed them:

" For more than forty years I have toiled
early and late to acquire independence and
ease for myself and my family.   To accom-
plish this, I became connected with some
English importing merchants in a seaport

town, and went largely into the English trade. Success crowned our endeavours; on balancing our acccunts two years ago, we found that our expectations were answered, and that we were now sufficiently wealthy to close business, which some proposed to do; it was, however, agreed to make one effort more, as some favourable circumstances appeared to offer, in which we adventured very largely, on a fair calculation of liberal and extensive proceeds.

" Before returns could be made, the war came on, embarrassments ensued, and by indubitable intelligence lately received, we find that our property in England has been sequestered; five of our ships, laden with English goods, lying in English harbours, and just ready to sail for America, have been seized as lawful prizes. Added to this, three vessels from the Indies, laden with island produce, have been taken on their homeward bound voyage, and one lost on her return from Holland. This wreck of fortune I might have survived, had I to sustain only my equal dividend of the loss : but of the merchants with whom I have been connected, not one remains to share the fate of the event; all have absconded or secreted themselves. To attempt to compound with my creditors would be of little avail ; my whole fortune will not pay one fourth of the debts; so that, compound or not, the consequence to me is inevitable ruin.

"To abscond would not secure me, as most of my remaining property is vested in real estate. And even if it would, I could not consent to it: I could not consent to banish myself from my country; to flee like a felon; to skulk from society with the base view of defrauding my creditors. No, I have lived honestly, and honestly will I die. By fair application and long industry my wealth has been obtained; and it shall never justly be said, that the reputation of my latter days was stained with acts of baseness and meanness. I have notified and procured a meeting of the creditors, and have laid the matters before them. Some appeared favourable to me; others insinuated that we were all connected in fraudulent designs, to swindle our creditors. This I repelled with becoming spirit, and was in consequence threatened with immediate prosecution. Whatever may be the event, I had some hopes that your happiness, Alonzo, might yet be secured. Hence I proposed your union with Melissa, before our misfortunes should be promulgated. Your parents are old; a little will serve the residue of their days. With your acquirements you may make your way in life. I shall have no property to give you; but I would still wish you to secure that which you prize far above, and without which, both honours and emoluments are unimportant and worthless."

At this moment a loud rap at the door interrupted the discourse, and three men were ushered in, which proved to be the sheriff and his attendants, sent by the more inexorable creditors of Alonzo's father and company, to level on the property of the former, which orders they faithfully executed, by seizing the lands, tenements and furniture, and finally arresting the body of the old gentleman, which was soon released by his friendly neighbours becoming bail for his appearance; but the property was soon after sold at public vendue, at less than half its value, and Alonzo's father and mother were compelled to abandon the premises, and take shelter in a little hut, belonging to a neighbouring farmer, illy and temporarily furnished by the gratuitous liberality of a few friends.

We will not stop the reader to moralize on this disastrous event. The feelings of the family can better be conceived than detailed. Hurled in a moment from the lofty summit of affluence to the low and barren vale of poverty! Philosophy came to the aid of the parents, but who can realise the feelings of the son! Thus suddenly cut short of his prospects, not only of future independence, but even of support, what would be the event of his suit to Melissa, and stipulated marriage? Was it not probable that her father would now cancel the contract? Could she consent to be his wife in his present penurious situation?— And indeed, could he himself consent to make her his wife, to make her miserable?

In this agitated frame of mind he received a letter from his friend in Melissa's neighbourhood, requesting him to come immediately to his house, whither he repaired the following day. This person had ever been the unchanging friend of Alonzo; he had heard of the misfortunes of his family, and he deeply sympathized in his distress. He had lately married and settled in life: his name was Vincent.

When Alonzo arrived at the house of his friend, he was received with the same disinterested ardour he ever had been in the day of his most unbounded prosperity.— After being seated, Vincent told him that the occasion of his sending for him was to propose the adoption of certain measures which he doubted not might be considered highly beneficial as it respected his future peace and happiness. "Your family misfortunes, continued Vincent, have reached the ears of Melissa's father. I know the old gentleman too well to believe he will consent to receive you as his son-in-law, under your present embarrassments. Money is the god to which he implicitly bows. The case is difficult, but not insurmountable. You must first see Melissa; she is now in the next room. I will introduce you in; converse with her, after which I will lay my plan before you."

Alonzo entered the room; Melissa was sitting by a window which looked into a pleasant garden, and over verdant meadows whose tall grass waved to the evening breeze. Farther on, low vallies spread their umbrageous thickets, where the dusky shadows of night had begun to assemble.

On high hills beyond, the tops of lofty forests, majestically moved by the billowy gales, caught the sun's last ray. Fleecy summer clouds hovered around the verge of the western horizon, spangled with silvery tints or fringed with the gold of evening.

A mournfully murmuring rivulet puried at a little distance from the garden, on the borders of a small grove, from whence the American wil l dove wafted her sympathetic moaning to the ear of Melissa. She sat leaning on a small table by the window, which was thrown up. Her attention was fixed. She did not perceive Vincent and Alonzo as they entered. They advanced

5   C

towards her. She turned, started, and a-
rose. With a melancholy smile, and tremulous voice, " I supposed, she said, that it
was Mrs. Vincent who was approaching, as
she has just left the room." Her countenance appeared dejected, which, on seeing
Alonzo, lighted up into a languid sprightliness. It was evident she had been weeping.

Vincent retired, and Alonzo and Melissa
seated themselves by the window. "I have
broken in upon your solitude, perhaps, too
unseasonably, said Alonzo. It is however,
the fault of Vincent:—he invited me to
walk into the room, but did not inform me
that you were alone." "Your presence was
sudden and unexpected, but not unseasoua-
ble, replied Melissa. I hope that you did
not consider any formality necessary in your
visits, Alonzo."

Alonzo. I once did not think so. Now
I know not what to think—I know not how
to act. You have heard of the misfortunes
of my father's family, Melissa?

Mel. Yes; I have heard the circumstances attending that event—an event in
which no one could be more deeply interested, except the immediate sufferers, than
myself.

Al. Your father is also acquainted with
my present situation?

Mel. He is.

Al.   How did he receive the intelligence?

Mel.   With deep regret.

Al.   And forbade you to admit my addresses any longer ?

Mel.   No, not absolutely.

Al.   If even in an unqualified or indirect
manner, it is proper I should know it.   .

Mel.   It certainly is.   Soon after we received the intelligence of your family misfortunes, my father came into the room
where I was sitting; " Melissa, said he,
your conduct has ever been that of a dutiful
child; mine, of an indulgent parent.—My
first, my ultimate wish, is to see my children, when settled in life, happy and honourably respected.   For this purpose, I have
bestowed on them a proper education, and
design suitably to apportion my property between them.   On their part, it is expected
they will act prudently and discreetly, especially in those things which concern their
future peace and welfare.—The principal
requisite to ensure this is a proper connex-
ion in marriage."   Here my father paused
a considerable time, and then continued—
" I know, my child, that your situation is a
very delicate one.   Your marriage day is
appointed ; it was appointed under the fairest prospects ; by the failure of Alonzo's
father, those prospects have become deeply
darkened, if not totally obliterated.

" To commit your fortune through life, to a person unable to support you, would be hazardous in the extreme. The marriage day can at least be suspended; perhaps something more favourable may appear.— At any rate, I have too much confidence in your discretion, to suppose that you will, by any rash act, bring either poverty or reproach upon yourself or your connexions." Thus spake my father, and immediately withdrew.

" In our present dilemma, said Alonzo what is proper to be done?"

It is difficult to determine, replied Melissa. Should my father expressly forbid our union, he will go all lengths to carry his commands into effect. Although a tender parent, he is violent in his prejudices, and resolute in his purposes. I would advise you to call at my father's house tomorrow, with your usual freedom. Whatever may be the event, I shall deal sincerely with you. Mr. and Mrs. Vincent are now my only confidants. From them you will be enable to obtain information, should I be debarred from seeing you. I am frequently here; they told me they expected you, but at what day was not known. Mrs. Vincent has been my friend and associate from my earliest years. Vincent you know. In

In them we can place the utmost confidence. My reliance on Providence, I
trust, will never be shaken; but my future prospects, at present, are dark and
gloomy."

" Let us not despair, answered Alonzo;
perhaps those gloomy clouds which now hover around us, will yet be dissipated by the
bright beams of joy. Innocence and virtue are the cares of Heaven. There lies my
hope. · To-morrow, as you propose, I will
call at you father's."

Melissa now prepared to return home; a
whippoorwill tuned its nightly song at a
little distance; but the sound, late so cheerful and sprightly, now passed heavily over
their hearts.

When Alonzo returned, Vincent unfolded the plan he had projected. "No sooner,
said he, was I informed of your misfortunes,
than I was convinced that Melissa's father
would endeavour to dissolve your intended
union with his daughter. I have known
him many years, and however he may dote
on his children, or value their happiness,
he will not hesitate to sacrifice his other
feelings to the acquirement of riches. It
appeared that you had but one resource left.
You and Melissa are now united by the
most solemn ties—by every rite except those
which are merely ceremonial. These I

5 *

would advise you to enter into, and trust to the consequences. Mrs. Vincent has proposed the scheme to Melissa; but implicitly accustomed to filial obedience, she shudders at the idea of a clandestine marriage. But when her father shall proceed to rigorous measures, she will, I think, consent to the alternative. And this measure, once adopted, her father must consent also; or, if not, you secure your own happiness, and, what you esteem more, that of Melissa."

" But you must be sensible of my inability to support her as she deserves, replied Alonzo, even should she consent to it."

The world is before you, answered Vin cent; you have friends, you have acquirements which will not fail you. In a country like this, you can hardly fail of obtaining a competency, which, with the other requisites, will ensure your independence and felicity."

Alonzo informed Vincent what had been agreed upon between Melissa and himself, respecting his visiting her on the morrow; " after which, he said, we will discourse further on the subject."

The next day Alonzo repaired to the house of Melissa's father. As he approached he saw Melissa sitting in a shady recess at one end of the garden near which the road passed. She was leaning with her

head upon her hand, in a pensive posture;
a deep dejection was depicted upon her features, which enlivened into a transient glow
as soon as she saw Alonzo. She arose, met
him, and invited him into the house.

Alonzo was received with a cool reserve
by all except Melissa. Her father saluted
him with a distant and retiring bow, as he
passed with Melissa to her room. As soon
as they were seated, a maiden aunt, who
had doubled her teens, outlived many of her
suiters, and who had lately come to reside
with the family, entered, and seated herself
by the window, alternately humming a tune
and impudently staring at Alonzo, without
speaking a word, except snappishly, to contra
dict Melissa in any thing she advanced, which
the latter passed off with only a faint smile.

. This interruption was not of long contin-
uance. Melissa's father entered, and requested the two ladies to withdraw, which
was instantly done. He then addressed A-
lonzo as follows :——"When I gave consent
for you to marry my daughter, it was on
the conviction that your future resources
would be adequate to support her honourably and independently. Circumstances
have since taken place, which render this
point extremely doubtful. Parental duty
and affection demand that I should know
your means and prospects before I sanction

a proceeding which may reduce my child to penury and to want."

He paused for a reply, but Alonzo was silent. He continued—"You yourself must acknowledge, that to burthen yourself with the expense of a family; to transfer a woman from affluence to poverty, without even an object in view to provide for either, would be the height of folly and extravagance." Again he paused, but Alonzo was still silent. He proceeded—"Could you, Alonzo, suffer life, when you see the wife of your bosom, probably your infant children, pining in misery for want of bread? And what else have you to expect if you marry in your present situation? You have friends and well wishers; but which of them will advance you four or five thousand pounds, as a gratuity? My daughter must be supported according to her rank and standing in life. Are you enabled to do this? If not, you cannot reasonably suppose that I shall consent to your marrying her. You may say that your acquirements, your prudence, and your industry, will procure you a handsome support. This well may do in single life; but to depend on these for the future exigencies of a family, is hazarding peace, honour and reputation, at a single game of chance. If, therefore, you have no resources or expectation

but such as these, your own judgment will
teach you the necessity of immediately re-
linquishing all pretensions to the hand of
Melissa"—and immediately left the room.

Why was Alonzo speechless through the
whole of this discourse?—What reply could
he have made? What were the prospects
before him but penury, want, misery, and
woe! Where, indeed, were the means by
which Melissa was to be shielded from poverty, if connected with his fortunes. The
idea was not new, but it came upon him
with redoubled anguish. He arose and
looked around for Melissa, but she was not
to be seen. He left the house, and walked
slowly towards Vincent's. At a little distance he met Melissa who had been strolling in an adjoining avenue. He informed
her of all that had passed; it was no more
than they both expected, yet it was a shock
their fortitude could scarcely sustain. Disappointment seldom finds her votaries prepared to receive her.

Melissa told Alonzo, that her father's determinations were unchangeable; that his
sister (the before mentioned maiden lady)
held a considerable influence over him, and
dictated the concerns of the family; and
that from her, there was nothing to hope in
their favour. Her mother, she said, was
her friend, but could not contradict the

will of her father.   Her brother would be
at home in a few days; how he would act
on this occasion she was unable to say : but
were he even their friend he would have
but feeble influence with her father and
aunt.   "What is to be the end of these
troubles, continued Melissa, it is impossible
to foresee.   Let us trust in the mercy of
heaven and submit to its dispensations."

Alonzo and Melissa, in their happier days,
had, when absent, corresponded by letters.
This method it was now thought best to
relinquish.   It was agreed that Alonzo
should come frequently to Vincent's, where
Melissa would meet him as she could find
opportunities.   Having concluded on this,
Melissa returned home, and Alonzo to the
house of his friend.

Vincent, after Alonzo had related the
manner of his reception at Melissa's father's, urged the plan he had projected of
a private marriage.   Alonzo replied, that
even should Melissa consent to it, which he
much doubted, it must be a measure of the
last resort, and adopted only when all others became fruitless.

The next morning Alonzo returned to the
hut where his aged parents now dwelt.   His
bosom throbbed with keen anguish.   His
own fate, unconnected with that of Melissa,
he considered of little consequence.   But

their united situation tortured his soul.—
What was to become of Melissa, what of
himself, what of his parents!—"Alas, said
Alonzo, I now perceive what it is to want
the good things of this life."

Alonzo's father was absent when he arrived, but returned soon after. A beam of
joy gleamed upon his withered countenance
as he entered the house. "Were it not,
Alonzo, for your unhappy situation, said he,
we should once more be restored to peace
and comfort. A few persons who were indebted to me, finding that I was to be sacrificed by my unfeeling creditors, reserved
those debts in their hands, and have now
paid me, amounting to something more
than five hundred pounds. With this I
have purchased a small, but well cultivated
farm, with convenient tenements. I have
enough left to purchase what stock and
other materials I need; and to spare some
for your present exigencies, Alonzo."

Alonzo thanked his father for his kindness, but told him that from his former
liberality he had yet sufficient for his wants,
and that he should soon find business which
would amply support him. " But your affair with Melissa, asked his father, how is
t' at likely to terminate?" " Favourably, I
h. e, sir," answered Alonzo. He could not

consent to disturb the tranquillity of his parents by reciting his own wretchedness.

A week passed away. Alonzo saw his
parents removed to their little farm, which
was to be managed by his father and a hir
ed man.   He saw them comfortably seated,
he saw them serenely blest in the calm
pleasures of returning peace, and a ray of
joy illuminated his troubled bosom.

> " Again the youth his wonted life regain'd,
> A transient sparkle in his eye obtain'd,
> A bright, impassion'd cheering glow, express'd
> The pleas'd sensation of his tender breast :
> But soon dark glooms the feeble smiles o'erspread ;
> Like morn's gay hues, the fading splendours fled ;
> Returning anguish froze his feeling soul,
> Deep sighs burst forth, and tears began to roll."

He thought of Melissa, from whom he
had heard nothing since he last saw her.—
He thought of the difficulties which surrounded him.   He thought of the barriers
which were opposed to his happiness and
the felicity of Melissa, and he set out for
the house of Vincent.

Alonzo arrived at the residence of Vincent near the close of the day.   Vincent
and his lady were at tea with several young
ladies who had passed the afternoon with
Mrs. Vincent.   Alonzo cast an active
glance around the company, in hopes to
find Melissa, but she was not there.   He
was invited and accepted a seat at table.
After tea Vincent led him into an adjoining

r)om.   "You have come in good time,
said he.   Something must speedily be done,
or you lose Melissa forever.   The day
after you were here, her father received a
letter from Beauman, in which, after mentioning the circumstance of your father's
insolvency. he hinted that the consequence
would probably be a failure of her proposed
marriage with you, which might essentially
injure the reputation of a lady of her standing in life; to prevent which, and to place
her beyond the reach of calumny. he offered to marry her at any appointed day, provided he had her free consent.

' As Beauman, by the recent death of
his father, had been put in possession of a
splendid fortune, the proposition allured her
father, who wrote him a complaisant answer, with an invitation to his house.—
He then strove to extort a promise from
Melissa, that she would break off all con-
nexion with you, see you no more, and admit the addresses of Beauman.

"To this she could not consent. She urged, that by the consent of her parents she
was engaged to you by the most sacred ties,
That to her father's will she had hitherto
yielded implicit obedience, but that hastily
to break the most solemn obligation, formed
and sanctioned by his approbation and direction, was what her conscience would not

permit her to do. Were he to command her to live single, life might be endured; but to give her hand to any except you, would be to perjure those principles of truth and justice which he himself had ever taught her to hold most inviolable.—Her father grew outrageous; charged her with disobedience, with a blind inconsiderate perverseness, by which she would bring ruin upon herself, and indelible disgrace upon her family. She answered only with her tears. Her mother interposed, and endeavoured to appease his anger; but he spurned her from him, and rushed out of the room, uttering a threat that force should succeed persuasion, if his commands were not obeyed. To add to Melissa's distress, Beauman arrived at her father's yesterday, and I hope, in some measure to alleviate it. Edgar, her brother, came this morning.— Mrs. Vincent has dispatched a message to inform Melissa of your arrival, and to desire her to come here immediately. She will undoubtedly comply with the invitation, if not prevented by something extraordinary. I should have written you had I not hourly expected you."

Mrs. Vincent now came to the door of the room and beckoned to her husband, who went out, but immediately returned, leading in Melissa after which he retired.

"Oh, Alonzo!" was all she could say, and burst into tears. Alonzo led her to a seat, gently pressed her hand, and mingled his tears with hers, but was unable to speak.—Recovering at length, he begged her to moderate her grief. "Where, said he, is your fortitude and your firmness, Melissa, which I have so often seen triumphing over affliction?" Her extreme anguish prevented a reply. Deeply affected and alarmed at the storm of distress which raged in her bosom, he endeavoured to console her, though consolation was a stranger to his own breast. "Let us not, Melissa, said he, increase our flood of affliction by a tide of useless sorrow. Perhaps more prosperous days are yet in reserve for us;—happiness may yet be ours." "Never, never! she exclaimed. Oh, what will become of me!" "Heaven cannot desert you, said Alonzo; as well might it desert its angels. This thorny and gloomy path may lead to fair fields of light and verdure. Tempests are succeeded by calms; wars end in peace; the splendours of the brightest morning arise on the wings of blackest midnight.——Troubles will not always last. Life at most is short. Death comes to the relief of the virtuous wretched, and transports them to another and better world, where sighing and sorrows cease,

and the tempestuous passions of life are
known no more."

The rage of grief which had overwhelmed Melissa began now to subside, as the
waves of the ocean gradually cease their
tumultuous commotion, after the turbulent
winds are laid asleep. Deep sobs and long
drawn sighs succeeded to a suffocation of
tears. The irritation of her feelings had
caused a more than usual glow upon her
cheek, which faded away as she became
composed, until a livid paleness spread itself over her features. Alonzo feared that
the delicacy of her constitution would fall
a sacrifice to the sorrow which preyed upon
her heart, if not speedily alleviated;—but
alas ! where were the means of alleviation ?

She informed him that her father had
that evening ordered her to become the
wife of Beauman. He told her that her
disobedience was no longer to be borne.—
" No longer, said he, will I tamper with
your perverseness : you are determined to
be poor, wretched and contemptible. I will
compel you to be rich, happy, and respected. You suffer the *Jack-a-lantern* fancy to
lead you into swamps and quagmires, when,
did you but follow the fair light of reason,
it would conduct you to honour and real
felicity. There are happiness and misery
at your choice.

"Marry Beauman, and you will roll in your coach, flaunt in your silks; your furniture and your equipage are splendid, your associates are of the first character, and your father rejoices in your prosperity.

"Marry Alonzo, you sink into obscurity, are condemned to drudgery, poorly fed, worse clothed, and your relations and acquaintances shun and 'despise you. The comparison I have here drawn between Beauman and Alonzo is a correct one; for even the wardrobe of the former is of more value than the whole fortune of the latter.

"I give you now two days to consider the matter; at the end of that time I shall expect your decision, and hope you will decide discretely. But remember that you become the wife of Beauman, or you are no longer acknowledged as my daughter."

"Thus, said Melissa, did my father pronounce his determination, which shook my frame, and chilled with horror every nerve of my heart, and immediately left me.

"My aunt added her taunts to his severities, and Beauman interfered with his ill-timed consolation. My mother and Edgar, ardently strove to allay the fever of my soul, and mitigate my distress. But the stroke was almost too severe for my nature. Habituated only to the smiles of my father, how could I support his frowns?—Accus-

6 *   D

tomed to receive his blessings alone, how
could I endure his sudden malediction."

Description would fail in painting the sen
sations of Alonzo's bosom, at this recital of
woe. But he endeavoured to mitigate her
sorrows by the consolation of more cheer-
ing prospects and happier hours.

Vincent and his lady now came into the
room. They strenuously urged the propriety
and the necessity of Alonzo and Melissa's
entering into the bands of wedlock immediately. "The measure would be hazardous,"
remarked Melissa. "My circumstances"—
said Alonzo. "Not on that account, interrupted Melissa, but my father's displeasure——" "Will be the same, whether
you marry Alonzo, or refuse to marry Beauman," replied Vincent. Her resolution appeared to be staggered.

"Come here, Melissa, to-morrow evening, said Mrs. Vincent; mean time you
will consider the matter, and then determine." To this Melissa assented, and prepared to return home.

Alonzo walked with her to the gate which
opened into the yard surrounding her father's house. It was dangerous for him to
go farther. Should he be discovered with
Melissa, even by a domestic of the family,
it must increase the persecutions against her.
They parted. Alonzo stood at the gate.

gazing anxiously after Melissa as she walked up the long winding avenue, bordered
with the odour-flowing lilac, and lofty elm,
her white robes now invisible, now dimly
seen as she turned the angles of the walk,
until they were totally obscured, mingling
with the gloom and darkness of the night.
"Thus, said Alonzo, thus fades the angel of
peace from the visionary eyes of the war-
worn soldier, when it ascends in the dusky
clouds of early morning, while he slumbers
on the field of recent battle."--With mournful forebodings he returned to the house of
Vincent. He arose after a sleepless nights
and walked into an adjoining field. He
stood leaning in deep contemplation against
a tree, when he heard quick footsteps behind him. He turned, and saw Edgar approaching : in a moment they were in each
other's arms, and mingled tears. They returned to Vincent's and conversed largely
on present affairs. " I have discoursed with
my father on the subject, said Edgar. I
have urged him with every possible argu-
ment to relinquish his determination : I fear,
however, he is inflexible.

"To assuage the tempest of grief which
rent Melissa's bosom was my next object,
and in this I trust I have not been unsuccessful. You will see her this evening, and
will find her more calm and resigned. You,

Alonzo, must exert your fortitude. The ways of Heaven are inscrutable, but they are right.

"We must acquiesce in its dealings. We cannot alter its decrees. Resignation to its will, whether merciful or afflictive, is one of those eminent virtues which adorn the good man's character, and ever find a brilliant reward in the regions of unsullied splendour, far beyond trouble and the tomb."

Edgar told Alonzo that circumstances compelled him that day to depart for the army. I would advise you, said he, to remain here until your affair comes to some final issue. It must, I think. ere long, be terminated. Perhaps you and my sister may yet be happy."

Alonzo feelingly expressed his gratitude to Edgar. He found in him that disinterested friendship, which his early youth had experienced. Edgar the same day departed for the army.

In the afternoon Alonzo received a note from Melissa's father, requesting his immediate attendance. Surprised at the incident, he repaired there immediately. The servant introduced him into a room where Melissa's father and aunt were sitting.——— " Hearing you were in the neighbourhood, said her father, I have sent for you, to make a proposition, which after what has taken place, I think you cannot hesitate to comply with. The occurrence of previous circumstances may lead you to suppose that my daughter is under obligations to you, which may render it improper for her to form marriage connections with any other. Whatever embarrassments your addresses to her may have produced, it is in your power to remove them; and if you are a man of honour you will remove them. You cannot wish to involve Melissa in your present penurious condition, unless you wish to make her wretched. It therefore only remains for you to give me a writing, voluntarily resigning all pretensions to the hand of my daughter; and if you wish her to be happy, honourable, and respected in this life, this I say you will not hesitate to do."

A considerable pause ensued. Alonzo at length replied, "I cannot perceive any particular advantage that can accrue from such a measure. It will neither add nor diminish the power you possess to command obedience to your will, if you are determined to command it, either from your daughter, or your servant."——

"There, brother," bawled the old maid, half squeaking through her nose, which was well charged with rappee, "did'nt I tell you so? I knew the fellow would not come to terms no more than will your refractory daughter. This love fairly bewitches such foolish, crack-brained youngsters. But say Mr. ——, what's your name, addressing herself to Alonzo, will love heat the oven? will love boil the pot? will love clothe the back? will love——"

"You will not, interrupted Melissa's father, speaking to Alonzo, it seems, consent to my proposition? I have then, one demand to make, which of right you cannot deny. Promise me that you will never see my daughter again, unless by my permission."

"At the present moment I shall promise you nothing," replied Alonzo, with some warmth.

"There again, said the old maid, just so Melissa told you this morning, when you requested her to see him no more. The fellow has fairly betwattled her. I wish I had him to deal with. Things wasn't so when I was a girl; I kept the rogues at a distance, I'll warrant you. I always told you, brother, what would come of your indulgence to your daughter. And I should not wonder if you should soon find the girl had eloped, and your desk robbed in the bargain."

Alonzo hastily arose: " I suppose, said he, my presence can be dispensed with."

" Well, young man, said Melissa's father,

since you will not comply with any over-
tures I make; since you will not accede to
any terms I propose, remember, sir, I now
warn you to break off all communication
and correspondence with my daughter, and
to relinquish all expectations concerning
her.   I snah never consent to marry my
daughter to a beggar."

"Beggar!" involuntarily exclaimed Alonzo, and his eyes flashed in resentment.--But
he recollected that it was the father of Melissa who had thus insulted him, and he sup-
pressed his anger.   He rushed out of the
house, and returned to Vincent's.   He had
neither heard nor seen any thing of Melissa
or Beauman.

Night came on, and he ardently and im-
patiently expected Melissa.   He anticipated the consolation her presence would bestow.   Edgar had told him she was more
composed.   He doubted whether it were
proper to excite anew her distress by rela-
ting his interview with her father, unless she
was appraised of it.   The evening passed
on, but Melissa came not.   Alonzo grew
restless and uneasy.   He looked out, then
at his watch.   Vincent and his lady assured
him that she would soon be there.   He paced the room.   Still he became more impa-
tient.   He walked out on the way where
she was expected to come.   Sometimes he

advanced hastily; at others he moved slowly; then stood motionless, listening in breathless silence, momentarily expecting to discover her white form approaching through
the gloom, or to hear the sound of her footsteps advancing amidst the darkness. Shape-
less objects, either real or imaginary, frequently crossed his sight, but, like the unreal phantoms of night, they suddenly passed
away, and were seen no more. At length
he perceived a dusky white form advancing
in the distant dim obscurity. It drew near;
his heart beat in quick succession; his fond
hopes told him it was Melissa. The object
came up, and hastily passed him, with a
" good night, sir."

It was a stranger in a white surtout. A-
lonzo hesitated whether to advance or to
eturn. It was possible, though not probable, that Melissa might have come some
other way. He hastened back to Vincent's
—she had not arrived. "Something extraordinary, said Mrs. Vincent, has prevented
her coming. Perhaps she is ill."—Alonzo
shuddered at the suggestion. He looked at
his watch; it was half past eleven o'clock.
Again he hastily sallied out, and took the
road to her father's.

The night was exceedingly dark, and illuminated only by the feeble glimmering of
the twinkling stars. When he came with-

in sight of the house, and as he drew near no lights were visible—all was still and silent. He entered the yard, walked up the avenue, and approached the door. The familiar watch-dog, which lay near the threshold, fawned upon him, joyfully whining and wagging his tail. "Thou still knowest me, Curlow, said Alonzo; thou hast known me in better days; I am now poor and wretched, but thy friendship is the same." A solemn stillness prevailed all around, interrupted only by the discordance of the nightly insects, and the hooting of the moping owl from the neighbouring forest.—The dwelling was shrouded in darkness. In Melissa's room no gleam of light appeared. "They are all buried in sleep, said Alonzo, deeply sighing, and I have only to return in disappointment."

He turned and walked towards the street; casting his eyes back, the blaze of a candle caught his sight. It passed rapidly along through the lower rooms, now gleaming, now intercepted, as the walls or the windows intervened, and suddenly disappeared. Alonzo gazed earnestly a few moments, and hastily returned back. No noise was to be heard, no new objects were discernible.— He clambered over the garden wall, and went around to the back side of the house. Here all wa solemn and silent as in front.

7

Immediately a faint light appeared through one of the chamber windows; it grew brighter; a candle entered the chamber; the sash was flung up, and Melissa seated herself at the window."

The weather was sultry, she held a fan in her hand; her countenance, though stamped with deep dejection, was marked with serenity, but pale as the drooping lily of the valley. Alonzo placed himself directly under the window, and in a low voice called her by name. She started wildly, looked out, and faintly cried, "Who's there?" He answered, "Alonzo." "Good heavens, she exclaimed, is it you, Alonzo? I was disappointe . in meeting you at Vincent's this evening; my father will not suffer me to go out without attendants. I am now constantly watched and guarded."

"Watched and guarded! replied Alonzo: At the risque of my life I will deliver you from the tyranny with which you are oppressed."

"Be calm, Alonzo, said she, I think it will not last long. Beauman will soon depart, after which there will undoubtedly be some alteration. Desire Mrs. Vincent to come here to-morrow; I believe they will let me see her. I can, from time to time, inform you of passing events, so that you may know what changes take place. I am placed under the care of my aunt, who suffers me not to step out of her sight. We pass the night in an adjoining chamber—from whence, after she had fallen asleep, I stole out, and went down with a design of walking in the garden, but found the doors all locked and the keys taken out. I returned and raised this window for fresh air. Hark! said she; my aunt calls me. She has waked and misses me. I must fly to her chamber. You shall hear more from me to-morrow by Mrs. Vincent, Alonzo." So saying, she let down the window sash, and retired.

Alonzo withdrew slowly from the place, and repassed the way he came. As he jumped back over the garden wall, he found a man standing at its foot, very near him: after a moment's scrutiny he perceived it to be Beauman. " What, my chevalier, said he to Alonzo, such an adept in the amorous science already? Hast thou then eluded the watchful eyes of Argus, and the vigilance of the dragon!"

" Unfeeling and impertinent intruder? retorted Alonzo, seizing hold of him; is it not enough that an innocent daughter must endure a merciless parent's persecuting hand, but must thou add to her misery by thy disgusting interference!"

" Quit thy hold, tarquin, said Beauman.

Art thou determined, after storming the fortress, to murder the garrison ?"

" Go, said Alonzo, quitting him ; go sir, you are unworthy of my anger. Pursue thy grovelling schemes. Strive to force to your arms a lady who abhors you, and were it not on one account, must ever continue to despise and hate you."

"Alonzo, replied Beauman, I perceive thou knowest me not. You and I were rivals in our pursuit—the hand of Melissa. Whether from freak or fortune, the preference was given to you, and I retired in silence. From coincidence of circumstances, her father has now been induced to give the preference to me. My belief was, that Melissa would comply with her father's will, especially after her prospects of connecting with you were cut off by the events which ruined your fortune. You, Alonzo, have yet, I find, to learn the character of women. It has been my particular study. Melissa, now ardently impassioned by first impressions, irritated by recent disappointment, her passions delicate and vivid, her affections animated and unmixed, it would be strange, if she could suddenly relinquish primitive attachments founded on such premises, without a struggle. But remove her from your presence for one year, with only distant and uncertain prospects of seeing you again, admit me as the substitute in your absence, and she accepts my hand as f ely as she would now receive yours. I haa no design—it was never my wish to marry her without her consent. That I believe I shall yet obtain. Under existing circumstances, it is impossible but that you must be separated for some considerable time. Then, when cool deliberation succeeds to the wild vagaries, the electric fire of frolic fancy, she will discover the dangerous precipice, the deadly abyss to which her present conduct and inclinations lead. She will see that the blandishments, without the possessions of life, must fade and die. She will discriminate between the shreds and the trappings of taste. She will prefer indifference and splendour to love and a cottage.

"At present I relinquish all further persuit; to-morrow I return to New-London. When Melissa, from calm deliberation and the advice of friends, shall freely consent to yield me her hand, I shall return to receive it. I came from my lodgings this evening to declare these intentions to her father: but it being later than I was aware of, the family had gone to rest. I was about to return, when I saw a light from the chamber window, which soon withdrew. I stood a moment by the garden wall, when you approached and discovered me." So saving, he bade Alonzo good night, and walked hastily away. " I find he knows not the character of Melissa," said Alonzo, and returned to Vincent's.

The next day Alonzo told the Vincents of all that had passed, and it was agreed that Mrs. Vincent should visit at Melissa's father's that afternoon. She went at an early hour. Alonzo's feelings were on the rack until she returned, which happened much sooner than was expected ; when she gave him and Vincent the following information :

"When I arrived there, said she, I found Melissa's father and mother alone, her mother was in tears, which she endeavoured to conceal. Her father soon withdrew. After some conversation I enquired for Melissa. The old lady burst into tears, and informed me that this morning Melissa's aunt (the old maid) had invited her to ride out with her. A carriage was provided, which, after a large trunk had been placed therein, drove off with Melissa and her aunt ; that Melissa's father had just been informing her that he had sent their daughter to a distant part of the country, where she was to reside with a friend until Alonzo should depart from the neighbourhood. The reason of this sudden resolution was his being informed by Beauman, that notwithstanding his precaution, Melissa and Alonzo had an interview the last evening. Where she was sent to, the old lady could not tell, but she was convinced that Melissa was not apprised of the design when she consented to go. Her aunt had heretofore been living with the relatives of the family in various parts of the state."

Alonzo listened to Mrs. Vincent's relation with inexpressible agitation. He sat silent a few moments; then suddenly starting up, " I will find her if she be on the earth!" said ne, and in spite of Vincent's attempts to prevent him, rushed out of the house, flew to the road, and was soon out of sight.

Melissa had not, indeed, the most distant suspicion of the designs of her father and aunt. The latter informed her that she was going to take a morning's ride, and invited Melissa to accompany her, to which she consented. She did not even perceive the trunk which was fastened on behind the carriage. They were attended by a single servant. They drove to a neighbouring town, where Melissa had frequently attended her father and mother to purchase articles of dress, &c. where they alighted at a friend's house, and lingered away the time until dinner; after which, they pre-

pared, as Melissa supposed, to return, but
found, to her surprise, after they had entered the carriage, that her aunt or lered the
driver to proceed a different way.   She asked her aunt if they were not going home.
" Not yet," said she.   Melissa grew uneasy ; she knew she was to see Mrs. Vincent
that afternoon ; she knew the disappointment which Alonzo must experience, if she
was absent.   She begged her aunt to return, as she expected the company of some
ladies that afternoon.   " Then they must
be disappointed, child," said her aunt.—
Melissa knew it was in vain to remonstrate;
she supposed her aunt was bent on visiting
some of her acquaintance, and she remained silent.

They arrived at another village, and a-
lighted at an inn, where Melissa and her
aunt tarried, while the servant was ordered
out by the latter on some business unknown
to Melissa.   When they again got into the
carriage she perceived several large packa-
ges and bundles, which had been deposited
there since they left it.   She enquired of
her aunt what they contained.   " Articles
for family use, child," she replied, and ordered the driver to proceed.

They passed along winding and solitary
paths, into a bye road which led through
an unfrequented wood, that opened into a

rocky part of the country bordering on the Sound. Here they stopped at the only house in view. It was a miserable hut, built of logs, and boarded with slabs. They alighted from the carriage, and Melissa's aunt, handing the driver a large bunch of keys, " remember to do as I have told you," said she, and he drove rapidly away. It was with some difficulty they got into the hut, as a meagre cow, with a long yoke on her neck, a board before her eyes, and a cross piece on her horns, stood with her head in the door. On one side of her were four or five half starved squeaking pigs, on the other a flock of gaggling geese.

As they entered the door, a woman who sat carding wool jumped up, " La me! she cried, here is Miss D——, welcome here again. How does madam do?" dropping a low curtsey. She was dressed in a linsey woolsey short gown, a petticoat of the same, her hair hanging about her ears, and barefoot. Three dirty, ragged children were playing about the floor, and the furniture was of a piece with the building. " Is my room in order?" enquired Melissa's aunt. " It hasn't been touched since madam was here," answered the woman, and immediately stalked away to a little back apartment, which Melissa and her aunt entered. It was small, but neatly furnished, and con-

E

tained a single bed. This appendage had been concealed from Melissa's view, as it was the opposite side of the house from whence she alighted. "Where is John?" asked Melissa's aunt. "My husband is in the garden, replied the woman; I will call him," and out she scampered. John soon appeared, and exhibited an exact counter part of his wife. "What does madam please to want?" said he, bowing three or four times. "I want you John," she answered, and immediately stepped into the other room, and gave some directions, in a low voice, to him and his wife. "La me! said the woman, madam a'nt a going to live in that doleful place?" Melissa could not understand her aunt's reply, but heard her give directions to "first hang on the tea-kettle." This done, while John and his wife went out, Melissa's aunt prepared tea in her own room. In about an hour John and his wife returned, and gave the same bunch of keys to Melissa's aunt, which she had given to the servant who drove the carriage.

Melissa was involved in inscrutable mystery respecting these extraordinary proceedings. She conjectured that they boded her no good, but she could not penetrate into her aunt's designs. She frequently looked out, hoping to see the carriage return, but was disappointed. When tea was made ready, she could neither eat nor drink. After her aunt had disposed of a dozen cups of tea, and an adequate proportion of biscuit, butter and dried beef, she directed Melissa to prepare to take a walk. The sun was low; they proceeded through fields, in a foot path, over rough and uneven ways, directly towards the Sound. They walked about a mile, when they came to a large, old fashioned, castle-like building, surrounded by a high, thick wall, and almost totally concealed on all sides from the sight, by irregular rows of large locusts and elm trees, dry prim* hedges, and green shrubbery. The gate which opened into the yard, was made of strong hard wood, thickly crossed on the outside with iron bars, and filled with old iron spikes. Melissa's aunt unlocked the gate, and they entered the yard, which was overgrown with rank grass and rushes : the avenue which led to the house was almost in the same condition. The house was of real Gothic architecture, built of rude stone, with battlements.

The doors were constructed in the same

*The botanical name of this shrub is not recollected. There were formerly a great number of prim hedges in New-England, and other parts of America. What is most remarkable i, that they all died the year previous to the commencement of the American war.

manner as the gate at which they entered the yard. They unlocked the door, which creaked heavily on its hinges, and went in. They ascended a flight of stairs, wound through several dark and empty rooms, till they came to one which was handsomely furnished, with a fire burning on the hearth. Two beds were in the room, with tables and chairs, and other conveniences for house keeping. " Here we are safe, said Melissa's aunt, as I have taken care to lock all the doors and gates after me ; and here, Melissa, you are in the mansion of your ancestors. Your great grand father, who came over from England, built this house in the earliest settlements of the country, and here he resided until his death. The reason why so high and thick a wall was built round it, and the doors and gates so strongly fortified, was to secure it against the Indians, who frequently committed depredations on the early settlers. Your grandfather came in possession of this estate after his father's death : it fell to me by will, with the lands surrounding it. The house has sometimes been tenanted, at others not. It has now been vacant for a few years. The lands are rented yearly. John, the person from whose house we last came, is my overseer and tenant. I had a small room built, adjoining that hut, where I gen-

erally i side for a week when I come to receive my rents. I have thought frequently
of fitting up this place for my future residence, but circumstances have hitherto hindered my carrying the scheme into effect,
and now, perhaps, it will never take place.
" Your perverseness, Melissa, in refusing
to comply with the wishes of your friends,
has indured us to adopt the method of
bringing you here, where you are to remain
until Alonzo leaves your neighbourhood, at
least. Notwithstanding your father's injunctions and my vigilance, you had a clandestine interview with him last night. So
we were told by Beauman this morning,
before he set off for New London, who discovered him at your window. It therefore
became necessary to remove you immediately. You will want for nothing. John
is to supply us with whatever is needful.—
You will not be long here; Alonzo will soon
be gone. You will think differently; return home, marry Beauman, and become a
lady."

" My God! exclaimed Melissa, is it possible my father can be so cruel! Is he so
unfeeling as to banish me from his house,
and confine me within the walls of a prison,
like a common malefactor?" She flung
herself on the bed in a state little inferior
to distraction. Her aunt told her it was

8

all owing to her own obstinacy, and because she refused to be made happy—and went to preparing supper.

Melissa heard none of her aunt's observations; she lay in a stupifying agony, insensible to all that passed. When supper was ready, her aunt endeavoured to arouse her. She started up, stared around her with a wild agonizing countenance, but spoke not a word. Her aunt became alarmed. She applied stimulants to her temples and forehead, and persuaded her to take some cordials. She remained seemingly insensible through the night: just at morning, she fell into a slumber, interrupted by incoherent moanings, convulsive startings, long drawn sighs, intermitting sobs, and by frequent, sudden and restless turnings from side to side. At length she appeared to be in a calm and quiet sleep for about an hour. About sunrise she awoke—her aunt sat by her bed side. She gazed languidly about the room, and burst into tears. She wept a long time; her aunt strove to console her, for she truly began to tremble, lest Melissa's distress should produce her immediate dissolution. Towards night, however, she became more calm and resigned; but a slight fever succeeded, which kept her confined for several days, after which she slowly recovered.

John came frequently to the house to receive the commands of Melissa's aunt, and brought such things as they wanted. Her aunt also sometimes went home with him, leaving the care of the house with Melissa, but locking one gate and taking the key of that with her. She generally returned before sunset. When Melissa was so far recovered as to walk out, she found that the house was situated on an eminence, about one hundred yards from the Sound. The yard was large and extensive. Within the enclosure was a spacious garden, now overrun with brambles and weeds. A few medicinal and odoriferous herbs were scattered here and there, and a few solitary flowers overtopped the tangling briars below; but there was plenty of fruit on the shrubbery and trees. The out buildings were generally in a ruinous situation. The cemetery was the most perfect, as it was built of hewn stone and marble, and had best withstood the ravages of time. The rooms in the house were mostly empty and decaying: the main building was firm and strong, as was also the extended wall which enclosed the whole. She found that although her aunt, when they first arrived, had led her through several upper rooms to the chamber they inhabited, yet there was from thence a direct passage to the hall.

The prospect was not disagreeable. West, all was wilderness, from which a brook wound along a little distance from the garden wall. North, were the uneven grounds she had crossed when she came there, bounded by distant groves and hills. East, beautiful meadows and fields, arrayed in flowery green, sloped to salt marshes or sandy banks of the Sound, or ended in the long white beaches which extended far into the sea. South, was the Sound of Long Island.

Melissa passed much of her time in tracing the ruins of this antiquated place, in viewing the white sails as they passed up and down the Sound, and in listening to the songs of the thousand various birds which frequented the garden and the forest. She could have been contented here to have buried her afflictions, and for ever to retire from the world, could Alonzo but have resided within those walls. " What will he think has become of me," she would say, while the disconsolate tear glittered in her eye. Her aunt had frequently urged her to yield to her father's injunctions, regain her liberty, and marry Beauman ; and she every day became more solicitous and impertinent. A subject so hateful to Melissa sometimes provoked her to tears ; at other her keen resentment. She therefore, when the weather was fair, passed much of her time in the garden and adjoining walks, wishing to be as much out of her aunt's company as possible.

One day John came there early in the morning, and Melissa's aunt went home with him. The day passed away, but she did not return. Melissa sat up until a late hour of the night, expecting her; she went to the gate, and found it was fast locked, returned, locked and bolted the doors of the house, went to bed and slept as soundly as she had done since her residence in the old mansion. "I have at least, she said, escaped the disgusting curtain-lecture about marrying Beauman."

The next day her aunt returned. "I was quite concerned about you, child, said she; how did you sleep?" "Never better, she answered, since I have been here." "I had forgotten, said her aunt, that my rents become due this week. I was detained until late by some of my tenants; John was out, and I dare not return in the night alone. I must go back to-day. It will take me a week to settle my business. If I am obliged to stay out again I will send one of John's daughters to sleep with you."——— "You need not give yourself that trouble, replied Melissa; I am under no apprehension of staying here alone; nothing can get

8 *

into or out of these premises."——Well,
thou hast wonderful courage, child, said her
aunt; but I shall be as frequently here as
possible, and as soon as my business is settled, I shall be absent no more." So saying, she bade Melissa good morning, and set
off for her residence at the dwelling of John.

She did not return in two days. The
second night of her absence, Melissa was
sitting in her chamber reading, when she
heard a noise as of several people trampling
in the yard below. She arose, cautiously
raised the window, and looked out. It was
extremely dark; she thought she might
have been discovered.

Her aunt came the next day, and told her
she was obliged to go into the country to
collect some debts of those to whom she
had rented lands: she should be gone a few
days, and as soon as she returned should
come there. "The keys of the house, said
she, I shall leave with you. The gate I
shall lock, and leave that key with John,
who will come here as often as necessary,
to assist you, and see if you want any thing."
She then went off, leaving Melissa not dis-
satisfied with the prospect of her absence.

Melissa amused herself in evenings by
reading in the few books her aunt had
brought there, and in the day, in walking
around the yard and garden, or in travers-

ing the rooms of the antique building. In
some, were the remains of ancient furniture,
others were entirely empty. Cobwebs and
mouldering walls were the principal ornaments left.

One evening as she was about retiring to
rest, she thought she heard the same trampling noise in the yard, as on a former occasion. She stepped softly to the window,
suddenly raised it, and held out the candle.
She listened and gazed with anxious solicitude, but discovered nothing more. All
was silent; she shut the window, and in a
short time went to bed.

Some time in the night she was suddenly
awakened by a sharp sound, apparently
near her. She started in a trembling panic, but endeavoured to compose herself
with the idea, that something had fallen
from the shelves. As she lay musing upon
the incident, she heard loud noises in the
rooms below, succeeded by an irregular and
confused number of voices, and presently
after, footsteps ascending the stairs which
led to her chamber. She trembled; a cold
chilly sweat run down her face. Directly
the doors below opened and shut with a
quick and violent motion. And soon after
she was convinced that she distinctly heard
a whispering in her room. She raised herself up in the bed and cast inquisitive eyes

towards her chamber door. All was darkness—no new object was visible—no sound
was heard, and she again lay down.

Her mind was too much agitated and a-
larmed to sleep. She had evidently heard
sounds, footsteps and voices in the house,
and whisperings which appeared to be in
her room. The yard gate was locked, of
which John had the key. She was confident that no person could ascend or get
over the wall of the enclosure. But if that
were practicable, how was it possible that
any human being could enter the house?
She had the key of every door, and they
were all fast locked, and yet she had heard
them furiously open and shut. A thought
darted into her mind,—was it not a plan
which her aunt had contrived in order to
frighten her to a compliance with her wishes? But then how could she enter the
house without keys? This might be done
with the use of a false key. But from
whence did the whisperings proceed, which
appeared close to her bedside? Possibly
it might be conveyed through the key-hole
of her chamber door. These thoughts tended in some degree, to allay her fears;—
they were possibilities, at least, however
improbable.

As she lay thus musing, a hand, cold as
the icy fingers of death, grasped her arm,

which lay on the outside of the bed clothes. She screamed convulsively, and sprang up in the bed. Nothing was to be seen—no noise was heard. She had not time to reflect. She flew out of the bed, ran to the fire, and lighted a candle. Her heart beat rapidly. She cast timid glances around the room, cautiously searching every corner, and examining the door. All things were in the same state she had left them when she went to bed. Her door was locked in the same manner ; no visible being was in the room except herself. She sat down, pondering on these strange events. Was it not probable that she was right in her first conjectures respecting their being the works of her aunt, and effected by her agents and instrumentality ? All were possible, except the cold hand which had grasped her arm. Might not this be the effect of a terrified and heated imagination ? Or if false keys had been made use of to enter the rooms below, might they not also be used to enter her chamber? But could her room be unlocked, persons enter, approach her bed, depart and re-lock the door, while she was awake, without her hearing them ?

She knew she could not go to sleep, and she determined not to go to bed again that night. She took up a book, but her spirits had been too much disordered by the past

scenes to permit her to read. She looked
out of the window. The moon had arisen
and cast a pale lustre over the landscape.
She recollected the opening and shutting of
the door—perhaps they were still open
The thought was alarming—She opened
her chamber door, and with the candle in
her hand, cautiously descended the stairs,
casting an inquisitive eye in every direction,
and stopping frequently to listen.—She advanced to the door; it was locked. She
examined the others; they were in the same
situation. She turned to go up stairs, when
a loud whisper echoed through the hall expressing "*away! away!*" She flew like
lightning to her chamber, relocked the door
and flung herself, almost breathless, into a
chair.

As soon as her scattered senses collected,
she concluded that whatever had been in
the house was there still. She resolved to
go out no more until day, which soon began to discolour the east with a fainter blue,
then purple streaks, intermingled with a
dusky whiteness, ascended in pyramidical
columns the zenith; these fading slowly
away, the eastern horizon became fringed
with the golden spangles of early morn. A
spot of ineffable brightness succeeded, and
immediately the sun burst over the verge

of creation, deluging the world in a flood of unbounded light and glory.

As soon as the morning had a little advanced, Melissa ventured out. She proceeded with hesitating steps, carefully scrutinizing every object which met her sight. She examined every door; they were all fast. She critically searched every room, closet, &c. above and below. She then took a light and descended into the cellar —here her inquisition was the same. Thus did she thoroughly and strictly examine and search every part of the house from the garret to the cellar, but could find nothing altered, changed, or removed; no outlet, no signs of there having been any being in the house the evening before, except herself.

She then unlocked the outer door and proceeded to the gate, which she found locked as usual. She next examined the yard, the garden, and all the out houses.

Nothing could be discovered of any person having been recently there. She next walked around by the wall, the whole circle of the enclosure. She was convinced that the unusual height of the wall rendered it impossible for any one to get over it. It was constructed of several tier of hewed timbers, and both sides of it were as smooth as glass. On the top, long spikes were thickly driven in, sharpened at both ends.

9

It was surrounded on the outside by a deep wide moat, which was nearly filled with water. Over this moat was a draw-bridge, on the road leading to the gate, which was drawn up, and John had the key.

The events of the past night, therefore, remained inscrutable. It must be that her aunt was the agent who had managed this extraordinary machinery.

She found John at the house when she returned. " Does madam want any thing to-day ?" asked he. "Has my aunt return-ed ?" enquired Melissa. " Not yet," he replied. " How long has she been gone ?" she asked. "Four days, replied Jonn, after counting his fingers, and she will not be back under four or five more." " Has the key of the gate been constantly in your possession ?" asked she. " The key of the gate and draw-bridge, he replied, have not been out of my possession for a moment since your aunt has been gone." "Has any person been to enquire for me or my aunt, she enquired, since I have been here ?"— " No, madam, said he, not a single person." Melissa knew not what to think ; she could not give up the idea of false keys—perhaps her aunt had returned to her father's.—Per-haps the draw-bridge had been let down, the gate opened, and the house entered by means of false keys. Her father would as soon do this as to confine her in this solitary place; and he would go all lengths to induce her, either by terror, persuasion or threats, to relinquish Alonzo and marry Beauman.

A thought impressed her mind which gave her some consolation. It was possible to secure the premises so that no person could enter even by the aid of false keys. She asked John if he would assist her that day. "In anything you wish, madam," he replied. She then directed him to go to work. Staples and iron bars were found in different parts of the building, with which he secured the doors and windows, so that they could be opened only on the inside. The gate, which swung in, was secured in the same manner. She then asked John if he was willing to leave the key of the gate and the draw-bridge with her. "Perhaps I may as well," said he; "for if you bar the gate and let down the bridge, I cannot get in myself until you let me in." John handed her the keys. "When I come," said he, "I will halloo, and you must let me in." This she promised to do, and John departed.*

That night Melissa let down the bridge,

* Of the place where Melissa was confined, as described in the foregoing pages, scarce a trace now remains. By the events of the revolution, the premises fell into other hands. The mansion, out houses and walls were torn down, the cemetery level-

locked and barred the gate, and the doors
and windows of the house : she also went
again over all parts of the building, strictly
searching every place, though she was well
convinced she should find nothing extraordinary.   She then retired to her chamber,
seated herself at a western window, and
watched the slow declining sun, as it leisurely sunk behind the lofty groves.   Pensive
twilight spread her misty mantle over the
landscape ;   the western horizon glowed
with the spangles of evening.   Deepening
glooms advanced.   The last beam of day
faded from the view, and the world was enveloped in night.   The owl hooted solemnly in the forest, and the whippoorwill sung
cheerfully in the garden.   Innumerable
stars glittered in the firmament, intermin-
ling their quivering lustre with the pale
splendours of the milky way.

Melissa did not retire from the window
until late ; she then shut it and withdrew
within the room.   She determined not to
go to bed that night.   If she was to be visited by beings, material or immaterial, she
chose not again to encounter them in darkness, or to be surprised when she was a-

---

led, the moat filled up; the locusts and elm trees were cut down;
all obstructions were removed, and the yard and garden converted into a beautiful meadow.   An elegant farm-house is now
erected on the place where John's hut then stood and the
neighbourhood is thinly settled.

sleep.   But why should she fear?   She
knew of none she had displeased except her
father, her aunt and Beauman.   If by any
of those the late terrifying scenes had been
wrought, she had now effectually precluded
a recurrence thereof, for she was well convinced that no human being could now enter the enclosure without her permission.
But if supernatural agents had been the actors, what had she to fear from them?   The
night passed away without any alarming
circumstances, and when daylight appeared
she flung herself upon the bed, and slept
until the morning was considerably advanced.   She now felt convinced that her former conjectures were right ; that it was
her aunt, her father, or both, who had caused the alarming sounds she had heard, a
repetition of which had only been prevented by the precautions she had taken.

When she awoke, the horizon was over-
clouded, and it began to rain.   It continued to rain until towards evening, when it
cleared away.   She went to the gate, and
found all things as she had left them : She
returned, fastened the doors as usual, examined all parts of the house, and again went
ing very drowsy, and convinced that she
was safe and secure, she went to bed ; leav-

ing, however, two candles burning in the
room.   As she, for two nights, had been deprived of her usual rest, she soon fell into a
slumber.

She had not long been asleep before she
was suddenly aroused by the apparent report of a pistol, seemingly discharged close
to her head.   Awakened so instantaneously, her recollection, for a time, was confused and imperfect.   She was only sensible
of a strong, sulphureous scent : but she soon
remembered that she had left two candles
burning, and every object was now shrouded in darkness.   This alarmed her exceedingly.   What could have become of the
candles ? They must have been blown out
or taken away.   What was the sound she
had just heard ?——What the sulphureous
stench which had pervaded the room ?——
While she was thus musing in perplexity, a
broad flash like lightning, transiently illuminated the chamber, followed by a long,
loud, and deep roar, which seemed to shake
the building to its centre.   It did not appear like thunder ; the sounds seemed to
be in the rooms directly over her head.
Perhaps, however, it was thunder.

Perhaps a preceding clap had struck near
the building, broken the windows, put out
the lights, and filled the house with the
electric effluvium.   She listened for a rep-

etition of the thunder—but a very different sound soon grated on her ear. A hollow, horrible groan echoed through her apartment, passing off in a faint dying murmur. It was evident that the groan proceeded from some person in the chamber. Melissa raised herself up in the bed; a tall white form moved from the upper end of the room, glided slowly by her bed, and seemed to pass off near the foot. She then heard the doors below alternately open and shut, slapping furiously, and in quick succession, followed by violent noises in the rooms below, like the falling of heavy bodies and the crash of furniture. Clamorous voices succeeded, among which she could distinguish boisterous menaces and threatenings, and the plaintive tone of expostulation.— A momentary silence ensued, when the cry of "*Murder! murder! murder!!*" echoed through the building, followed by the report of a pistol, and shortly after, the groans of a person apparently in the agonies of death, which grew fainter and fainter until it died away in a seemingly expiring gasp. A dead silence prevailed for a few minutes, to which a loud hoarse peal of ghastly laughter succeeded—then again all was still. But she soon heard heavy footsteps ascending the stairs to her chamber door. It was now she became terrified and

9 *

alarmed beyond any former example.——
" Gracious heaven, defend me ! she exclaimed; what am I coming to !"   Knowing
that every avenue to the enclosure was effectually secured; knowing that all the
doors and windows of the house, as also that
which opened into her chamber, were fast
locked, strictly bolted and barred ; and
knowing that all the keys were in her possession, she could not entertain the least
doubt but the noises she had heard were
produced by supernatural beings, and, she
had reason to believe, of the most mischiev-
ous nature.   She was now convinced that
her father or her aunt could have no agency in
the business.   She even wished her aunt
had returned.   It must be exceedingly difficult to cross the moat, as the draw bridge
was up; it must be still more difficult to
surpass the wall of the enclosure ; it was
impossible for any human being to enter
the house, and still more impossible to enter her chamber.

While she lay thus ruminating in extreme agitation, momentarily expecting to
have her ears assailed with some terrific
sound, a pale light dimly illuminated her
chamber.   It grew brighter.   She raised
herself up to look towards the door ;—the
first object which met her eye, was a most
horrible form, standing at a little distance

from her bedside. Its appearance was tall
and robust, wrapped in a tattered white
.obe, spotted with blood. The hair of its
head was matted with clotted gore. A
deep wound appeared to have pierced its
breast, from which fresh blood flowed down
its garment. Its pale face was gashed and
gory! its eyes fixed, glazed, and glaring;—
its lips open, its teeth set, and in its hand
was a bloody dagger.

Melissa, uttering a shriek of terror,
shrunk into the bed, and in an instant the
room was involved in pitchy darkness. A
freezing ague seized her limbs, and drops of
chilling sweat stood upon her face. Immediately a horrid hoarse voice burst from a-
midst the gloom of her apartment, *" Begone!
begone from this house!"* The bed on
which she lay then seemed to be agitated,
and directly she perceived some person
crawling on its foot. Every consideration,
except present safety, was relinquished; instantaneously she sprang from the bed to
the floor—with convulsed grasp, seized the
candle, flew to the fire and lighted it. She
gazed wildly around the room—no new object was visible. With timid step she approached the bed; she strictly searched all
around and under it, but nothing strange
could be found. A thought darted into her
mind to leave the house immediately and

fly to John's : this was easy, as the keys of the gate and draw-bridge were in her possession. She stopped not to reconsider her determination, but seizing the keys, with the candle in her hand, she unlocked her chambe⁻ door, and proceeded cautiously down stairs, fearfully casting her eyes on each side, as she tremblingiy advanced to the outer door. She hesitated a moment. To what perils was she about to expose herself, by thus venturing out at the dead of the night, and proceeding sueh a distance alone? Her situation she thought could become no more hazardous, and she was about to unbar the door, when she was alarmed by a deep, hollow sigh. She looked around and saw, stretched on one side of the hall, the same ghastly form which had so recently appeared standing by her bedside. The same haggard countenance, the same awful appearance of murderous death. A faintness came upon her; she turned to flee to her chamber—the candle dropped from her trembling hand, and she was shrouded in impenetrable darkness. She groped to find the stairs: as she came near their foot, a black object, apparently in human shape, stood before her, with eyes which seemed to burn like coals of fire, and red flames issuing from its mouth. As she stood fixed a moment in inexpressible trepidation, a large ball of fire rolled along the hall, towards the door, and burst with an explosion which seemed to rock the building to its deepest foundation.   Melissa closed her eyes and sunk senseless to the floor. She revived and got to her chamber, she hardly knew how ; locked her door, lighted another candle, and after again searching the room, flung herself into a chair, in a state of mind which almost deprived her of reason.

Daylight soon appeared, and the cheerful sun darting its enlivening rays through the crevices and windows of the antique mansion, recovered her exhausted spirits, and dissipated, in some degree, the terrors which hovered about her mind.   She endeavoured to reason coolly on the events of the past night, but reason could not elucidate them.   Not the least noise had been heard since she last returned to her chamber: she therefore expected to discover no traits which might tend to a disclosure of those mysteries.   She consoled herself only with a fixed determination to leave the desolate mansion.   Should John come there that day, he might be prevailed on to permit her to remain at her aunt's apartment in his house until her aunt should return.   If he should not come before sunset, she resolved to leave the mansion and proceed there.

She took some refreshment and went down stairs : she found the doors and windows all fast as she had left them. She then again searched every room in the house, both above and below, and the cellar; but she discovered no appearance of there having been any person there. Not the smallest article was displaced; every thing appeared as it had formerly been.— She then went to the gate; it was locked as usual, and the draw-bridge was up. She again traversed the circuit of the wall, but found no alteration, or any place where it was possible the enclosure might be entered. Again she visited the outer buildings, and even entered the cemetery, but discovered not the least circumstance which could conduce to explain the surprising transactions of the preceding night. She however returned to her room in a more composed frame of spirit, confident that she should not remain alone another night in that gloomy, desolate, and dangerous solitude.

Towards evening Melissa took her usual walk around the enclosure. It was that season of the year when weary summer is lapsing into the arms of fallow autumn.— The day had been warm, and the light gales bore revigorating coolness on their wings as they tremulously agitated the foliage of the western forest, or fluttered among the branches of the trees surrounding the mansion. The green splendours of spring had begun to fade into a yellow lustre, the flowery verdure of the fields was changed to a russet hue. A robin chirped on a neighbouring oak, a wren chattered beneath, swallows twittered around the decayed buildings, the ludicrous mocking bird sung sportively from the top of the highest elm and the surrounding groves rung with varying, artless melody; while deep in the adjacent wilderness the woodcock, hammering on some dry and blasted trees, filled the woods with reverberant echoes. The Sound was only ruffled by the lingering breezes, as they idly wandered over its surface. Long Island, now in possession of the British troops, was thinly enveloped in smoky vapour; scattered along its shores lay the numerous small craft and larger ships of the hostile fleet. A few skiffs were passing and repassing the Sound, and several American gun-boats lay off a point which jutted out from the main land, far to the eastward. Numberless summer insects mingled their discordant strains amidst the weedy herbage. A heavy black cloud was rising in the north west, which seemed to portend a shower, as the sonorous, distant thunder was at long intervals distinctly heard.

Melissa walked around the yard, contemplating the varying beauties of the scene: the images of departed joys—the days when Alonzo had participated with her in admiring the splendours of rural prospects, raised in her bosom the sigh of deep regret. She entered the garden and traversèd the alleys, now overgrown with weeds and tufted knot-grass. The flower beds were choaked with the low running bramble and tangling five-finger; tall, rank rushes, mullens and daisies, had usurped the empire of the kitchen garden. The viny arbour was broken, and principally gone to decay; yet the " lonely wild rose" blushed mournfully amidst the ruins. As she passed from the garden she involuntarily stopped at the cemetery : she paused in serious reflection: —" Here, said she, in this house of gloom rest, in undisturbed silence, my honourable ancestors, once the active tenants of yonder mansion. Then, throughout these solitary demesnes, the busy occurrences of life glided in cheerful circles. Then, these now moss-clad alleys, and this wild weedy garden, were the resort of the fashionable and the gay. Then, evening music floated over the fields, while yonder halls and apartments shone in brilliant illumination. Now all is sad, solitary and dreary, the haunt of spirits and spectres of nameless terror. All that now remains of the head that formed, the hand that executed, and the bosom that relished this once happy scenery, is now, alas, only a heap of dust."

She seated herself on a little hillock, under a weeping willow, which stood near the cemetery, and watched the rising shower, which ascended in gloomy pomp, half hidden behind the western groves, shrouding the low sun in black vapour, while coming thunders more nearly and more awfully rolled. The shrieking night hawk* soared high into the air, mingling with the lurid van of the approaching storm, which widening, nore rapidly advanced, until "the heavens were arrayed in blackness."

The lightning broader and brighter flashes, hurling down its forky streaming bolts far in the wilderness, its flaming path followed by the vollying artillery of the skies. Now bending its long, crinkling spires over the vallies, now glimmering along the summit of the hills. Convolving clouds poured smoky volumes through the expansion; a deep, hollow, distant roar, announced the approach of " summoned winds." The whole forest bowed in awful grandeur, as from its dark bosom rushed the impetuous hurricane, twisting off, or tearing up

*Supposed to be the male whippoorwill; well known in the N.w-England states, and answering to the above peculiarity.

by the roots, the stoutest trees, whirling
the heaviest branches through the air with
irresistible fury. It dashed upon the sea,
tossed it into irregular mountains, or mingled its white foamy spray with the gloom
of the turbid skies. Slant-wise, the large
heavy drops of rain began to descend. Melissa hastened to the mansion; as she reached the door a very brilliant flash of lightning, accompanied by a tremendous explosion, alarmed her. A thunder bolt had entered a large elm tree within the enclosure,
and with a horrible crash, had shivered it
from top to bottom. She unlocked the
door and hurried to her chamber. Deep
night now filled the atmosphere; the rain
poured in torrents, the wind rocked the
building, and bellowed in the adjacent
groves: the sea raged and roared, fierce
lightnings rent the heavens, alternately in-
volving the world in the sheeted flame of
its many coloured fires; thunders rolled
awfully around the firmament, or burst
with horrid din, bounding and reverberat-
ing among the surrounding woods, hills and
vallies. It seemed nothing less than the
crash of worlds sounding through the uni-
verse.

Melissa walked her room, listening to the
wild commotion of the elements. She feared that if the storm continued, she should

be compelled to pass another night in the lone mansion : if so, she resolved not to go to bed.   She now suddenly recollected that in her haste to regain her chamber, she had forgotten to lock the outer door.   The shock she had received when the lightning demolished the elm tree, was the cause of this neglect.   She took the candle, ran hastily down, and fastened the door.   As she was returning, she heard footsteps, and imperfectly saw the glance of something coming out of an adjoining room into the hall.   Supposing some ghastly object was approaching, she averted her eyes and flew to the stairs.   As she was ascending them, a voice behind her exclaimed, " Gracious heaven ! Melissa !"   The voice agitated her frame with a confused, sympathetic sensation.   She turned, fixed her eyes upon the person who had spoken ; unconnected ideas floated a moment in her imagination : " Eternal powers ! she cried, it is Alonzo."

Alonzo and Melissa were equally surprised at so unexpected a meeting.   They could scarcely credit their own senses.— How he had discovered her solitude—what led him to that lonely place—how he had got over the wall—were queries which first arose in her mind.   He likewise could not conceive by what miracle he should find her in a remote, desolate building, which he had supposed to be uninhabited. With rapture he took her trembling hand; tears of joy choaked their utterance. "You are wet, Alonzo, said Melissa at length; we will go up to my chamber; I have a fire there, where you can dry your clothes."——"Your chamber; replied Alonzo, who then inhabits this house?" "No one except myself, she answered; I am here alone, Alonzo." "Alone! he exclaimed—here alone, Melissa! Good God! tell me how—why—by what means are you here alone?" "Let us go up to my chamber, she replied, and I will tell you all."

He followed her to her apartment and seated himself by the fire. "You want refreshment," said Melissa—which was indeed the case, as he had been long without any, and was wet, hungry and weary.

She immediately set about preparing tea and soon had it ready, and a comfortable repast was spread for his entertainment.—And now, reader, if thou art a child of nature, if thy bosom is susceptible of refined sensibility, contemplate for a moment, Melissa and Alonzo seated at the same table, a table prepared by her own hand, in a lonely mansion, separated from society, and no one to interrupt them. After innumerable difficulties, troubles and perplexities; after vexing embarrassments, and a cruel separa

tion, they were once more together, and
for some time every other consideration
was lost. The violence of the storm had
not abated. The lightning still blazed, the
thunder bellowed, the wind roared, the sea
raged, the rain poured, mingled with heavy
hail . Alonzo and Melissa heard a little of it.
She told him all that had happened to her
since they parted, except the strange noises
and awful sights which had terrified her
during her confinement in that solitary
building : this she considered unnecessary
and untimely, in her present situation.

Alonzo informed her, that as soon as he
had learned the manner in which she had
been sent away, he left the house of Vincent and went to her father's to see if he
could not find out by some of the domes-
tics what course her aunt had taken. None
of them knew any thing about it. He did
not put himself in the way of her father, as
he was apprehensive of ill treatment thereby. He then went to several places among
the relatives of the family where he had
heretofore visited with Melissa, most of
whom received him with a cautious cold-
ness. At length he came to the house of
Mr. Simpson, the gentleman to whose seat
Alonzo was once driven by a shower, where
he accidentally found Melissa on a visit, as
mentioned before. Here he was admitted

10 *   G

with the ardour of friendship. They had
heard his story : Melissa had kept up a correspondence with one of the young ladies ;
they were therefore informed of all, except
Melissa's removal from her father's house :
of this they knew nothing until told thereof by Alonzo.

"I am surprised at the conduct of my
kinsman, said Mr. Simpson ; for though his
determinations are, like the laws of the
Medes and Persians, unalterable, yet I have
ever believed that the welfare of his children lay nearest his heart. In the present
instance he is certainly pursuing a mista
ken policy. I will go and see him." He
then ordered his horse, desiring Alonzo to
remain at his house until he returned.

Alonzo was treated with the most friendly politeness by the family ; he found that
they were deeply interested in his favour
and the welfare of Melissa. At evening
Mr. Simpson returned. " It is in vain, said
he, to reason with my kinsman; he is determined that his daughter shall marry your
rival. He will not even inform me to what
place he has sent Melissa. Her aunt however is with her, and they must be at the
residence of some of the family relatives.—
I will despatch my son William among
connections, to see if he can find her

The next morning William depart

was gone two days; but could not obtain the least intelligence either of Melissa or her aunt, although he had been the rounds among the relations of the family.

"There is some mystery in this affair, said Mr. Simpson. I am very little acquainted with Melissa's aunt. I have understood that she draws a decent support from her patrimonial resources, which, it is said, are pretty large, and that she resides alternately with her different relatives. I have understood also that my kinsman expects her fortune to come into his family, in case she never marries, which, in all probability, she now will not, and that she, in consequence, holds considerable influence over him. It is not possible but that Melissa is yet concealed at some place of her aunt's residence, and that the family are in the secret. I think it cannot be long before they will disclose themselves: You, Alonzo, are welcome to make my house your home; and if Melissa can be found, she shall be treated as my daughter."

Alonzo thanked him for his friendship and fatherly kindness. "I must continue, said he, my researches for Melissa; the result you shall know."

He then departed, and travelled through the neighbouring villages and adjoining

neighbourhoods, making, at almost every
house, such enquiries as he considered necessary on the occasion.   He at length arrived at the inn in the last little village
where Melissa and her aunt had stopped
the day they came to the mansion.   Here
the inn-keeper informed him that two ladies, answering his description, had been at
his house : he named the time, which was
the day in which Melissa, with her aunt,
left her father's house.   The inn-keeper
told him that they purchased some articles
in the village, and drove off to the south.
Alonzo then traversed the country adjoining the Sound, far to the westward, and
was returning eastward, when he was overtaken by the shower.   No house being
within sight, be betook himself to the forest for shelter.   From a little hilly glade
in the wilderness, he discovered the lonely
mansion which, from its appearance, he very naturally supposed to be uninhabited.—
The tempest soon becoming severe, he
thought he would endeavour to reach the
house.

   When he arrived at the moat, he found
it impossible to cross it, or ascend the wall;
and he stood in momentary jeopardy of his
life, from the falling timber, some of which
was broken and torn up by the tornado, and
some splintered by the fiery bolts of hea-

ven. At length a large tree, which stood near him, on the verge of the moat, or rather in that place, was hurled from its foundation, and fell, with a hideous crash, across the moat, its top lodging on the wall. He scrambled up on the trunk, and made his way on the wall. By the incessant glare of lightning he was able to see distinctly. The top of the tree was partly broken by the force of its fall, and hung down the other side of the wall. By these branches he let himself down into the yard, proceeded to the house, found the door open, which Melissa had left in her fright, and entered into one of the rooms, where he proposed to stay until at least the shower was over, still supposing the house unoccupied, until the noise of locking the door, and the light of the candle, drew him from the room, when, to his infinite surprise, he discovered Melissa, as before related.

Melissa listened to Alonzo with varied emotion. The fixed obduracy of her father, the generous conduct of the Simpsons, the constancy of Alonzo, filled her heart with inexpressible sensations. She foresaw that her sufferings were not shortly to end—— she knew not when her sorrows were to close.

Alonzo was shocked at the alteration which appeared in the features of Melissa.

The rose had faded from her cheek, except when it was transiently suffused with a hectic flush. A livid paleness sat upon her countenance, and her fine form was rapidly wasting. It was easy to be foreseen that the grief which preyed upon her heart would soon destroy her, unless speedily allayed.

The storm had now passed into the regions of the east; the wind and rain had ceased, the lightning more unfrequenily flashed, and the thunder rolled at a distance. The hours passed hastily;—day would soon appear. Hitherto they had been absorbed in the present moment; it was time to think of the future. After the troubles they had experienced; after so fortunate a meeting, they could not endure the idea of another and immediate separation. And yet immediately separated they must be. It would not be safe for Alonzo to stay even until the rising sun, unless he was concealed; and of what use could it be for him to remain there in concealment?

In this dilemma there was but one expedient. "Suffer me, said Alonzo to Melissa, to remove you from this solitary confinement. Your health is impaired. To you, your father is no more a father; he has steeled his bosom to paternal affection; he has banished you from his house, placed you under the tyranny of others, and confined you in a lonely, desolate dwelling, far from the sweets of society; and this only because you cannot heedlessly renounce a most solemn contract, formed under his eye, and sanctioned by his immediate consent and approbation. Pardon me, Melissa, I would not censure your father; but permit me to say, that after such treatment, you are absolved from implicit obedience to his rigorous, cruel, and stern commands.—It will therefore be considered a duty you owe to your preservation, if you suffer me to remove you from the tyrannical severity with which you are oppressed."

Melissa sighed, wiping a tear which fell from her eye. "Unqualified obedience to my parents, said she, I have ever considered the first of duties, and have religiously practised thereon——but where, Alonzo, would you remove me?" "To any place you shall appoint," he answered. "I have no where to go," she replied.

If you will allow me to name the place, said he, I will mention Mr. Simpson's. He will espouse your cause and be a father to you, and, if conciliation is possible, will reconcile you to your father. This can be done without my being known to have any agency in the business. It can seem as if

Mr. Simpson had found you out. He will go any just lengths to serve us. It was his desire, if you could be found, to have you brought to his house. There you can remain either in secret or openly, as you shall choose. Be governed by me in this, Melissa, and in all things I will obey you thereafter. I will then submit to the future events of fate; but I cannot Melissa—I cannot leave you in this doleful place."

Melissa arose and walked the room in extreme agitation. What could she do? She had, indeed, determined to leave the house, for reasons which Alonzo knew nothing of. But should she leave it in the way she had proposed, she was not sure but she would be immediately remanded back, more strictly guarded, and more severely treated. To continue there, under existing circumstances, would be impossible, long to exist. She therefore came to a determination—"I will go, she said, to Mr. Simpson's."

It was then agreed that Alonzo should proceed to Vincent's, interest them in the plan, procure a carriage, and return at eleven o'clock the next night. Melissa was to have the draw-bridge down, and the gate open. If John should come to the house the succeeding day, she would persuade him to let her still keep the keys. But it was possible her aunt might return. This would render the execution of the scheme more hazardous and difficult. A signal was therefore agreed on; if her aunt should be there, a candle was to be placed at the window fronting the gate, in the room above; if not, it was to be placed against a similar window in the room below. In the first case Alonzo was to rap loudly at the door. Melissa was to run down, under pretence of seeing who was there, fly with Alonzo to the carriage, and leave her aunt to scrape acquaintance with the ghosts and 'goblins of the old mansion. For even if her aunt should return, which was extremely doubtful, she thought she could contrive to let down the bridge and unlock the gate in the evening without her knowledge. At any rate she was determined not to let the keys go out of her hands, unless they were forced from her, until she had escaped from that horrid and dreary place.

Daylight began to break from the east, and Alonzo prepared to depart. Melissa accompanied him to the gate and the bridge, which was let down: he passed over, and she slowly withdrew, both frequently turning to look back. When she came to the gate, she stopped;—Alonzo stopped also. She waved a white handkerchief she had in her hand, and Alonzo bowed in answer to the sign. She then leis-

11

urely entered and slowly shut the gate.—
Alonzo could not forbear climbing up into
a tree to catch another glimpse of her as
she passed up the avenue. With lingering
step he saw her move along, soon receding
from his view in the gray twilight of misty
morning. He then descended, and hastily
proceeded on his journey.

Traits of glory now painted the eastern
skies. The glittering day-star, having unbarred the portals of light, began to trens-
mit its retrocessive lustre. Thin scuds flew
swiftly over the moon's decrescent form.
Low, hollow winds, murmured among the
bushes, or brushed the limpid drops from
intermingling foliage. The fire-fly* sunk,
feebly twinkling, amidst the herbage of the
fields. The dusky shadows of night fled to
the deep glens, and rocky caverns of the
wilderness. The American lark soared high
in the air, consecrating its matin lay to
morn's approaching splendours. The woodlands began to ring with native melody—
the forest tops, on high mountains, caught
the sun's first ray, which, widening and ex-
tending, soon gem'd the landscape with
brilliants of a thousand various dies.

As Alonzo came out of the fields near
the road, he saw two persons passing in an
open chair. They suddenly stopped, earn-

* The American lampyris, vulgarly called the lightning-bug.

es y gazing at him. They were wrapped
in long riding cloaks, and it could not be
distinguished from their dress whether they
were men or women. He stood not to notice them, but made the best of his way to
Vincent's, where he arrived about noon.
—Rejoiced to find that he had discovered
Melissa, they applauded the plan of her removal, and assisted him in obtaining a carriage. A sedan was procured, and he sat
out to return, promising to see Vincent a-
gain, as soon as he had removed Melissa to
Mr. Simpson's. He made such use of his
time as to arrive at the mansion at the
hour appointed. He found the draw-bridge
down, the gate open, and saw, as had been
agreed upon, the light at the lower window,
glimmering through the branches of trees.
He was therefore assured that Melissa was
alone. His heart beat; a joyful tremor
seized his frame; Melissa was soon to be
under his care, for a short time at least.—
He drove up to the house, sprang out of
the carriage, and fastened his horse to a lo-
cust tree: The door was open; he went
in, flew lightly up stairs, entered her chamber—Melissa was not there! A small fire
was blazing on the hearth, a candle was
burning on the table. He stood petrified
with amazement, then gazed around in
anxious solicitude. What could have be-

come of her? It was impossible, he tho't, but that she must still be there..

Had she been removed by fraud or force, the signal candle would not have been at the window. Perhaps, in a freakish moment, she had concealed herself for no other purpose than to cause him a little perplexity. He therefore took the candle and searched every corner of the chamber, and every room of the house, not even missing the garret and the cellar. He then placed the candle in a lantern, and went out and examined the out-houses: he next went round the garden and the yard, strictly exploring and investigating every place; but he found her not. He repeatedly and loudly called her by name; he was answered only by the solitary echoes of the wilderness.

Again he returned to the house, traversed the rooms, there also calling on the name of Melissa : his voice reverberated from the walls, dying away in solemn murmurs in the distant empty apartments. Thus did he continue his anxious scrutiny, alternately, in the house and the enclosure, until day-- but no traces could be discovered, nothing seen or heard of Melissa. What had become of her he could not form the most distant conjecture. Nothing was removed from the house; the beds, the chairs, the table, all the furniture remained in the same condition as when he was there the night before;—the candle, as had been a-greed upon, was at the window, and a nother was burning on the table :—it was therefore evident that she could not have been long gone when he arrived. By what means she had thus suddenly disappeared, was a most deep and inscrutable mystery.

When the sun had arisen, he once more repeated his inquisitive search, but with the same effect.   He then, in extreme vex-ation and disappointment, flung himself in-to the sedan, and drove from the mansion. Frequently did he look back at the build-ing, anxiously did he scrutinize every sur-rounding and receding object.   A thrill of pensive recollection vibrated through his frame as he passed the gate, and the keen agonizing pangs of blasted hope, pierced his heart, as his carriage rolled over the bridge.

Once more he cast a "longing, lingering look" upon the premises behind, sacred on-ly for the treasure they lately possessed; then sunk backward in his seat, and was dragged slowly away.

Alonzo had understood from Melissa, that John's hut was situated about one mile north from the mansion where she had been confined.   When he came out near the road, he left his horse and carriage, after securing them, and went in search of it.—

11 *

He soon discovered it, and knew it from the description given thereof by Melissa. —He went up and knocked at the door, which was opened by John, whom Alonzo also knew, from the portrait Melissa, had drawn of him.

John started in amazement. "Understanding, said Alonzo, that you have the charge of the old mansion in yonder field, I have come to know if you can inform me what has become of the young lady who has been confined there."

"Confined! answered John, I did not know she was confined."

Recollecting himself, "I mean the young lady who has lately resided there with her aunt," replied Alonzo.

"She was there last night, answered John; her aunt is gone into the country and has not returned."

Alonzo then told him the situation of the mansion, and that she was not there. John informed him that she was there about sunset, and according to her request he had left the keys of the gate and bridge with her : he desired Alonzo to tarry there until he ran to the mansion.

He returned in about half an hour. "She is gone, sure enough, said John ; but how, or where, it is impossible for me to guess."
—Convinced that he knew nothing of the

matter, Alonzo left him and returned to
Vincent's.

Vincent and his lady were much surprised at Alonzo's account of Melissa's sudden
disappearance, and they wished to ascertain whether her father's family knew any
thing of the circumstance.   Social inter-
course had become suspended between the
families of Vincent and Melissa's father, as
the latter had taxed the former of improperly endeavouring to promote the views of
Alonzo.   They therefore procured a neighbouring woman to visit Melissa's mother,
to see if any information could be obtained
concerning Melissa; but the old lady had
heard nothing of her since her departure
with her aunt, who had never yet returned.
—Alonzo left Vincent's and went to Mr.
Simpson's.   He told them all that had happened since he was there, of which, before,
they had heard nothing.   At the houses of
Mr. Simpson and Vincent he resided some
time, while they made the most dilligent
search to discover Melissa; but nothing
could be learned of her fate.

Alonzo then travelled into various parts
of the country, making such enquiries as
caution dictated of all whom he thought
likely to give him information;—but he
found none who could give him the least
intelligence of his ost Melissa.

In the course of his wanderings he passed near the old mansion house where Melissa had been confined. He felt an inclination once more to visit it: he proceeded
over the bridge, which was down, but he
found the gate locked. He therefore hurried back and went to John's, whom he
found at home. On enquiring of John whether he had yet heard any thing of the
young lady and her aunt; ''All I know of
the matter, said John, is, that two days after you were here, her aunt came back with
a strange gentleman, and ordered me to go
and fetch the furniture away from the room
they had occupied in the old mansion. I
asked her what had become of young madam. She told me that young madam had
behaved very indiscreetly, and she found
fault with me for leaving the keys in her
possession, though I did not know that any
harm could arise from it. From the discourse which my wife and I afterwards
overheard between madam and the strange
gentleman, I understood that young madam
had been sent to reside with some friend or
relation at a great distance, because her
father wanted her to marry a man, and she
wishes to marry somebody else.'' From
John's plain and simple narrative, Alonzo
concluded that Melissa had been removed
by her father's order, or through the agen-

cy, or instigation of her aunt. Whether his visit to the old mansion had been somehow discovered or suspected, or whether she was removed by some preconcerted or anteced- ent plan, he could not conjecture.—Still, the situation in which he found the mansion the night he went to convey her away, left an inexplicable impression on his mind. He could in no manner account how the candle could be placed at the window according to agreement, unless it had been done by her- self; and if so, how had she so suddenly been conveyed away?

Alonzo asked John where Melissa's aunt now was.

"She left here yesterday morning, he an- swered, with the strange gentleman I men- tioned, on a visit to some of her friends."

"Was the strange gentleman you speak of her brother?" asked Alonzo.

"I believe not, replied John, smiling and winking to his wife;—I know not who he was; somebody that madam seems to like pretty well."

"Have you the care of the old mansion?" said Alonzo.

"Yes, answered John, I have the keys; I will accompany you thither, perhaps you would like to purchase it; madam said yes- terday she thought she should sell it."

Alonzo told him he had no thoghts of

H

purchasing, thanked him for his information, and departed.

Convinced now that Melissa was removed by the agency of her persecutors, he compared the circumstances of John's relation. "She had been sent to reside with some friend or relation at a great distance." This great distance, he believed to be New London, and her friend or relation, her cousin, at whose house Alonzo first saw her, under whose care she would be safe, and Beauman would have an opportunity of renewing his addresses. Under these impressions, Alonzo did not long hesitate what course to pursue—he determined to repair to New London immediately.

In pursuance of his design he went to his father's. He found the old gentleman with his man contentedly tilling his farm, and his mother cheerfully attending to household affairs, as their narrow circumstances would not admit her to keep a maid without embarrassment. Alonzo's soul sickened on comparing the present state of his family with its former affluence; but it was an unspeakable consolation to see his aged parents contented and happy in their humble situation; and though the idea could not pluck the thorn from his own bosom, yet it tended temporarily to assuage the anguish of the wound.

"You have been long gone, my son, said his father; I scarcely knew what had become of you.   Since I have become a farmer I know little of what is going forward in the world; and indeed we were never happier in our lives.   After stocking and paying for my farm, and purchasing the requisites for my business, I have got considerable money at command: we live frugally, and realize the blessings of health, comfort, and contentment.   Our only disquietude is on your account, Alonzo.   Your affair with Melissa, I suppose, is not so favourable as you could wish.   But despair not, my son; hope is the harbinger of fairer prospects: rely on Providence, which never deserts those who submissively bow to the justice of its dispensations."

Unwilling to disturb the serenity of his parents, Alonzo did not tell them his troubles.   He answered, that perhaps all might yet come right; but that, as in the present state of his mind he thought a change of situation might be of advantage, he asked liberty of his father to travel for some little time.   To this his father consented, and offered him a part of the money he had on hand, which Alonzo refused, saying he did not expect to be long gone, and his resources had not failed him.

He then sold off his books, his horses,

his carriages, &c. the *insignia* of his better days, but now useless appendages, from which he raised no inconsiderable sum.—He then took a tender and affectionate leave of his parents, and set out for New London.

Alonzo journeyed along with a heavy heart and in an enfeebled frame of spirits. Through disappointment, vexation, and the fatigues he had undergone in wandering a-bout, for a long time, in search of Melissa, despondency had seized upon his mind, and indisposition upon his body. He put up the first night within a few miles of New Haven, and as he passed through that town the next morning, the scenes of early life in which he had there been an actor, moved in melancholy succession over his mind. That day he grew more indisposed; he experienced an unusual languor, listlessness and debility; chills, followed by hot flashes, heavy pains in the head and back, with incessant and intolerable thirst. It was near night when he reached Killingsworth, where he halted, as he felt unable to go farther: he called for a bed, and through the night was racked with severe pain, and scorched with a burning fever.

The next morning he requested that the physician of the town might be sent for;—he came and ordered a prescription which give his patient some relief; and by strict attention, in about ten days Alonzo was able to pursue his journey. He arrived at New London, and took lodgings with a private family of the name of Wyllis, in a retired part of the town.

The first object was to ascertain whether Melissa was at her cousin's. But how should he obtain this information? He knew no person in the town except it was those whom he had reason to suppose were leagued against him. Should he go to the house of her cousin, it might prove an injury to her if she were there, and could answer no valuable purpose if she were not. —The evening after he arrived there he wrapped himself up in his cloak and took the street which led to the house of Melissa's cousin: he stopped when he came against it, to see if he could make any discoveries. As people were passing and repassing the street, he got over into a small enclosure which adjoined the house, and stood under a tree, about thirty yards from the house: he had not long occupied this station, before a lady came to the chamber window, which was flung up, opposite to the place where he stood; she leaned out, looked earnestly around for a few minutes, then shut it and retired. She had brought a candle into the room, but did not bring it

to the window; of course he could not distinguish her features so as to identify them.

He knew it was not the wife of Melissa's
cousin, and from her appearance he believed it to be Melissa.   Again the window
opened, again the same lady appeared;—
she took a seat at a little distance within
the room; she reclined with her head upon
her hand, and her arm appeared to be supported by a stand or table.   Alonzo's heart
beat violently, he now had a side view of
her face, and was more than ever convinced that it was Melissa.   Her delicate features, though more pale and dejected than
when last he saw her;—her brown hair,
which fell in artless circles around her lily
neck; her arched eye-brows and commanding aspect.   Alonzo moved towards the
house, with a design, if possible, to draw
her attention, and should it really prove to
be Melissa, to discover himself.   He had
proceeded but a few steps before she arose,
shut the window, retired, and the light disappeared.   Alonzo waited a considerable
time, but she appeared no more.   Supposing she had retired for the night, he slowly withdrew, chagrined at this disappointment, yet pleased at the discovery he had
made.

The family with whom Alonzo had taken lodgings were fashionable and respecta-

ble. The following afternoon they had appointed to visit a friend, and they invited Alonzo to accompany them. When they named the family where their visit was intended, he found it to be Melissa's cousin. Alonzo therefore declined going under pretence of business. He however waited with anxiety for their return, hoping he should be able to learn by their conversation, whether Melissa was there or not.— When they returned he made some enquiries concerning the families in town, until the conversation turned upon the family they had visited. "The young lady who resides there, said Mrs. Wyllis, is undoubtedly in a confirmed decline; she will never recover."

Alonzo started, deeply agitated. "Who is the young lady?" he asked. "She is sister to the gentleman's wife where we visited, answered Mr. Wyllis;—her father lives in Newport, and she has come here for her health." "Do you not think, said Mrs. Wyllis, that she resembles their cousin Melissa, who resided there some time ago?" "Very much indeed, replied her husband, only she is not quite so handsome."

Again was Alonzo disappointed, and again did he experience a melancholy pleasure: he had the last night hoped that he had discovered Melissa, but to find her in a hopeless decline, was worse than that she should remain undiscovered.

"It is reported, said Mrs. Wyllis, that Melissa has been upon the verge of matrimony, but that the treaty was somehow broken off; perhaps Beauman will renew his addresses again, should this be the case." ".Beauman has other business besides addressing the ladies, answered Mr. Wyllis. He has marched to the lines near New-York with his new raised company of volunteers."*

From this discourse, Alonzo was convinced that Melissa was not the person he had seen at her cousin's the preceding evening, and that she was not there. He also found that Beauman was not in town. Where to search next, or what course to pursue, he was at a loss to determine.

The next morning he rose early and wandered about the town. As he passed by the house of Melissa's cousin, he saw the lady, who had appeared at the window, walking in the garden. Her air, her figure, had very much the appearance of Melissa; but the lineaments of her countenance were, when viewed by the light of day, widely dissimilar. Alonzo felt no strong curiosity farther to examine her features, but passing on, returned to his lodgings.

* New-York was then in possession of the British troops.

How he was now to proceed, Alonzo could not readily decide. To return to his native place, appeared to be as useless as to tarry where he was. For many weeks had he travelled and searched every place where he thought it probable Melissa might be found, both among her relatives and elsewhere. He had made every effort to obtain some clue to her removal from the old mansion, but he could learn nothing but what he had been told by John. If his friends should ever hear of her, they could not inform him thereof, as no one knew where he was. Would it not, therefore, be best for him to return back, and consult with his friends, and if nothing had been heard of her, pursue some other mode of enquiry? He might, at least, leave directions where his friends might write to him, in case they should have any thing whereof to apprise him.

An incident tended to confirm this resolution. He one night dreamed that he was sitting in a strange house, contemplating on his present situation, when Melissa suddenly entered the room. Her appearance was more pale, sickly and dejected, than when he last saw her. Her elegant form had wasted away, her eyes were sunk, her cheeks fallen, her lips livid. He fancied it to be night, she held a candle in her hand,

12 *

smiling languidly upon him;—she turned
and went out of the room, beckoning him
to follow : he thought he immediately arose
and followed her.   She glided through several winding rooms, and at length he lost
sight of her, and the light gradually fading
away, he was involved in deep darkness.—
He groped along, and at length saw a faint
distant glimmer, the course of which he
pursued, until he came into a large room,
hung with black tapestry, and illuminated
by a number of bright tapers.   On one side
of the room appeared a hearse, on which
some person was laid : he went up to it—
the first object that arrested his attention
was the lovely form of Melissa, shrouded in
the sable vestments of death ! Cold and
lifeless, she lay stretched upon the hearse,
beautiful even in dissolution; the dying
smile of complacency had not yet deserted
her cheek.   The music of her voice had
ceased; her fine eyes had closed for ever.
Insensible to objects in which she once de-
lighted; to afflictions which had blasted
her blooming prospects, and drained the
streams of life, she lay like blossomed trees
of spring, overthrown by rude and boisterous winds.   The deep groans which convulsed the distracted bosom, and shocked
the trembling frame of Alonzo, broke the
delusive charm : he awoke, rejoiced to find

it but a dream, though it impressed his mind
with doleful and portentous forebodings.

It was a long time before he could again
close his eyes to sleep; he at length fell
into a slumber, and again he dreamed. He
fancied himself with Melissa, at the house
of her father, who had consented to their
union, and that the marriage ceremony between them was there performed. He
thought that Melissa appeared as she had
done in her most fortunate and sprightly
days, before the darts of adversity, and the
thorns of affliction, had wounded her heart.
Her father seemed to be divested of all his
awful sternness, and gave her to Alonzo
with cheerful freedom. He awoke, and the
horrors of his former dream were dissipated
by the happy influences of the last.

"Who knows, he said, but that this may
finally be the case; but that the sun of
peace may yet dispel the glooms of these
distressful hours!" He arose, determined
to return home in a few days. He went
out and enjoyed his morning walk in a more
composed frame of spirits than he had for
some time experienced. He returned, and
as he was entering the door he saw the
weekly newspaper of the town, which had
been published that morning, and which the
carrier had just flung into the hall.——The
family had not yet arisen. He took up the

paper, carried it to his chamber, and opened it to read the news of the day.   He ran his eye hastily over it, and was about to lay it aside, when the death list arrested his attention, by a display of broad black lines. The first article he read therein was as follows :

"Died, of a consumption, on the 26th ult. at the seat of her uncle. Col. W. D—, near Charleston, South Carolina, whither she had repaired for her health, Miss Melissa D——, the amiable daughter of J—— D——, Esq. of *******, Connecticut, in the eighteenth year of her age."

The paper fell from the palsied hand—a sudden faintness came upon him—the room grew dark—he staggered, and fell senseless upon the floor.

The incidents of our story will here produce a pause.——The fanciful part of our readers may cast it aside in chagrin and disappointment.   "Such an event," may they say, "we were not prepared to expect.— After so many, and such various trials of heart; after innumerable difficulties surmounted; almost invincible objects overcome, and insuperable barriers removed— after attending the hero and heroine of your tale through the diversified scenes of anxiety, suspense, hope, disappointment, expectation, joy, sorrow, anticipated bliss, sudden and disastrous woe——after elevating them to the threshold of happiness, by the premature death of one, to plunge the other, instantaneously, in deep and irretrievable despair, must not, cannot be right.—Your story will hereafter become languid and spiritless; the subject will be uninteresting, the theme unengaging, since the *genius* which animated and enlivened it is gone for ever."

Reader of sensibility, stop. Are we not detailing facts? Shall we gloss them over with false colouring? Shall we describe things as they are, or as they are not? Shall we draw with the pencil of nature, or of art? Do we indeed paint life as it is, or as it is not? Cast thine eyes, reader, over the ephemeral circle of passing and fortuitous events; view the change of contingencies; mark well the varied and shifting scenery in the great drama of time;—seriously contemplate nature in her operations; minutely examine the entrance, the action, and the exit of characters on the stage of existence—then say, if disappointment, distress, misery and calamitous woe, are not the inalienable portion of the susceptible bosom. Say, if the possession of refined feeling is enviable——the lot of *Nature's children* covetable—whether to such, through life, the sprinklings of comfort are sufficient to give a zest to the bitter banquets of adversity—whether, indeed, sorrow, sighing, and tears, are not the inseparable attendants of all those whose hearts are the repositories of tender affections and pathetic sympathies.

But what says the moralist?—" Portray life as it is. Delude not the senses by deceptive appearances. Arouse your hero? call to his aid stern philosophy and sober reason. They will dissipate the rainbow-glories of unreal pleasure, and banish the glittering meteors of unsubstantial happiness. Or if these fail, lead him to the holy fane of religion: she will regulate the fires of fancy, and assuage the tempest of the passions: she will illuminate the dark wilderness, and smooth the thorny paths of life: she will point him to joys beyond the tomb —to *another and a better world* ; and pour the balm of consolation and serenity over his wounded soul."

Shall we indeed arouse Alonzo? Alas! to what paths of grief and wretchedness shall we arouse him! To a world to him void and cheerless—a world desolate, sad and dreary.

Alonzo revived. " Why am I, he exclaimed, recalled to this dungeon of torment? Why was not my spirit permitted to take its flight to regions where my guardian is gone? Why am I cursed with memory? O that I might be blessed with forgetfulness! But why do I talk of blessings?—Heaven never had one in store for me. Where are fled my anticipated joys? To the bosom the dark bosom of the oblivious tomb! There lie all the graces worthy of love in life—all the virtues worthy of lamentation in death! There lies perfection; perfection has here been found. Was she not all that even heaven could demand?—Fair, lovely, holy and virtuous. Her tender solicitudes, her enrapturing endearments, her soul-inspiring blandishments,—gone, gone for ever? That heavenly form, that discriminate mind—all lovely as light, all pure as a seraph's—a prey to worms—mingled with incorporeal shadows, regardless of former inquietudes or delights, regardless of the keen anguish which now wrings tears of blood from my despairing heart!

"Eternal Disposer of events! if virtue be thy special care, why is the fairest flower in the garden of innocence and purity blasted like a noxious weed? Why is the bright gem of excellence trampled in the dust like a worthless pebble?—Why is Melissa hurried to the tomb?"

Thus raved Alonzo. It was evident that delirium had partially seized his brain. He arose and flung himself on the bed in un-

speakable agony. "And what, Alas! he
again exclaimed, now remains for me? Existence and unparalleled misery. The consolation even of death is denied me. But
Melissa! she—ah, where is she! Ob, reflection insupportable! insufferable consideration! Must that heavenly frame putrify,
moulder, and crumble into dust? Must the
loathsome spider nestle on her lily bosom?
the odious reptile riot on her delicate limbs?
the worm revel amid the roses of her cheek,
fatten on ner temples, and bask in the lustre of her eyes? Alas! the lustre has become dimmed in death: the rose and the
lily are withered; the harmony of her voice
has ceased; the graces, the elegancies of
form, the innumerable delicacies of air, all
are gone, and I am left in a state of misery
which defies mitigation or comparison."

Exhausted by excess of grief, he now lay
in a stupifying anguish, until the servant
summoned him to breakfast. He told the
servant he was indisposed and requested he
might not be disturbed. Mr. Wyllis and
his lady came up, anxious to yield him any
assistance in their power, and advised him
to call a physician. He thanked them, but
told them it was unnecessary; he only wanted rest. His extreme distress of mind
brought on a relapse of fever, from which
he had but imperfectly recovered. For seve

ral days he lay in a very dangerous and doubtful state. A physician was called, contrary to his choice or knowledge, as for most part of the time his mind was delirious and sensation imperfect. This was, probably the cause of baffling the disorder. He was in a measure insensible to his woes. He did not oppose the prescriptions of the physician. The fever abated; nature triumphed over disease of body, and he slowly recovered, but the malady of his mind was not removed.

He contemplated on the past. "I fear, said he, I have murmured against the wisdom of Providence. Forgive, O merciful Creator! Forgive the frenzies of distraction!" He now recollected that Melissa once told him that she had an uncle who resided near Charleston in South Carolina; thither he supposed she had been sent by her father, when she was removed from the old mansion, in order to prevent his having access to her, and with a view to compel her to marry Beauman. Her appearance had indicated a deep decline when he last saw her. "There, said he, far removed from friends and acquaintance, there did she languish, there did she die—a victim to excessive grief, and cruel parental persecution."

As soon as he was able to leave his room,

13   I

he walked out one evening, and in deep
contemplation roved, he knew not where.
The moon shone brilliantly from her lofty
throne; the chill, heavy dews of autumn
glittered on the decaying verdure. The
*cadeal** croaked hoarsely among the trees;
the *dirclet* sung mournfully on the grass.—
Alonzo heard them not; he was insensible
to all external objects, until he had imper-
ceptibly wandered to the rock on the point
of the beach, verging the Sound, to which
he had attended Melissa the first time he
saw her at her cousin's.‡ Had the whole
artillery of Heaven burst, in sheeted flame,
from the skies—had raging winds mingled
the roaring waves with the mountains—
had an instantaneous earthquake burst beneath his feet, his frame would not have
been so shocked, his soul so agitated!—
Sudden as the blaze darts from the electric
cloud was he aroused to a lively sense of
blessings entombed! The memory of departed joys passed with rapidity over his
imagination; his first meeting with Melis-
a; the evening he had attended her to

---

*† Lcal names given to certain American insects, from their
sound. They are well known in various parts of the United
States; generally make their appearance about the latter end
of August, and continue until destroyed by the frost. The
notes of the first are hoarse, sprightly, and discordant; the
last, solemn and mournfully pleasing.

‡ See page 8. See also allusions to this scene in several sub-
sequent parts of the story.

that place; her frequent allusions to the scenery there displayed, when they had traversed the fields, or reclined in the bower on her favourite hill;.in fine, all the vicissitudes through which they had passed, were called to his mind. His fancy saw her—felt her gently leaning on his arm, while he tremblingly pressed her hand.—Again he saw smiling health crimsoning the lilies of her cheek; again he saw the bright soul of sympathetic feelings sparkling in her eye; the air of ease; the graces of attitude; her brown locks circling the borders of her snowy robe. Again he was enraptured by the melody of her voice.—Once more would he have been happy, had not fancy changed the scene. But, alas! she shifted the curtain. He saw Melissa stretched on the sable hearse, wrapped in the dreary vestments of the grave; the roses withered; the lilies faded; motionless; the graces fled; her eyes fixed, and sealed in the glaze of death! Spontaneously he fell upon his knees, and thus poured forth the overcharged burden of his anguished bosom.

"Infinite Ruler of all events! Great Sovereign of this ever changing world! Omnipotent Controler of vicissitudes! Omniscient dipenser of destinies! The beginning, the progression, the end is thine. Unsearchable are thy purposes! mysterious thy movements! inscrutable thy operations! An atom of thy creation, wildered in the mazes of ignorance and woe, would bow to thy decrees. Surrounded with impenetrable gloom, unable to scrutinize the past, incompetent to explore the future —— fain would he say, THY WILL BE DONE! And Oh, that it might be consistent with that HIGH WILL to call *this atom* from a dungeon of wretchedness, to worlds of light and glory, where his only CONSOLATION is gone."

Thus prayed the heart-broken Alonzo. It was indeed a worldly prayer; but perhaps as pure and as acceptable as many of our modern professors would have made on a similar occasion. He arose and repaired to his lodgings. One determination only he had now fallen upon—to bury himself and his griefs from all with whom he had formerly been acquainted. Why should he return to the scenes of his former bliss and anxiety, where every countenance would tend to renew his mourning; where every door would be inscribed with a *memento mori*, and where every object would he shrouded in crape? He therefore turned his attention to the army; but the army was far distant, and he was too feeble to prosecute a journey of such an extent.

There were at that time preparations

for fitting out a convoy, at private expense, from various parts of the United States, for the protection of our European trade; they were to rendezvous at a certain station, and thence proceed with the merchantmen under their care to the ports of France and Holland, where our trade principally centered, and return as convoy to some other mercantile fleet.

One of these ships of war was then nearly fitted out at New-London. Alonzo offered himself to the captain, who, pleased with his appearance, gave him the station of commander of marines.

Alonzo prepared himself with all speed for the voyage. He sought, he wished no acquaintance. His only place of resort, except to his lodgings and the ship, was to Melissa's favourite rock : there he bowed as to the shrine of her spirit, and there he consecrated his devotions.

As he was one day passing through the town, a gentleman stepped out of an adjoining house and accosted him. Alonzo immediately recognized him to be the cousin of Melissa, at whose house he had first seen her. He was dressed in full mourning, which was a sufficient indication that he was apprised of her death. He invited Alonzo to his house, and he could not complaisantly refuse the invitation. He there-

13 *

fore accepted it, and passed an hour with
him, from whom he learnt that Melissa had
been sent to her uncle's at Charleston, for
the recovery of her health, where she died.
" Her premature death. said her cousin, has
borne so heavily upon her aged father, that
it is feared he will not long survive."——
" Well may it wring his bosom, thought A-
lonzo;——his conscience can never be at
peace." Whether Melissa's cousin had been
informed of the particulars of Alonzo's unfortunate attachment, was not known, as he
instituted no conversation on the suɒject.
Oeither did he enquire into Alonzo's prospects; he only invited him to call again.
Alonzo thanked him, but replied it would
be doubtful, as he should shortly leave town.
He made no one acquainted with his intentions.

The day at length arrived when the ship
was to sail, and Alonzo to leave the shores
of America.   They spread their canvass to
propitious gales; the breezes rushed from
their woody coverts, and majestically wafted them from the harbour.

Slowly the land receded; fields, forests,
hills, mountains, towns and villages leisurely withdrew, until they were mingled in one
common mass.   The ocean opening, ex-
panded and widened, presenting to the astonished eyes of the untried mariner its

wilderness of waters. Near sunset, Alonzo ascended the mast to take a last view of a country once so dear, but whose charms were now lost forever. The land still appeared like a simicircular border of dark green velvet on the edge of a convex mirror. The sun sunk in fleecy golden vapours behind it. It now dwindled to discoloured and irregular spots, which appeared like objects floating, amidst the blue mists of distance, on the verge of the main, and immediately all was lost beneath the spherical, watery surface.

Alonzo had fixed his eyes, as near as his judgment could direct, towards Melissa's favourite rock, till nothing but sea was discoverable. With a heart-parting sigh he then descended. They had now launched into the illimitable world of billows, and the sable wings of night brooded over the boundless deep.

A new scene was now opened to Alonzo in the wonders of the mighty deep. The sun rising from and setting in the ocean; the wide-spread region of watery waste, now snooth as polished glass, now urged into irregular rolling hillocks, then swelled to

Blue trembling billows, topp'd with foam,"

or gradually arising into mountainous waves. Often would he traverse the deck amid the still hours of midnight, when the moon sil-

vered over the liquid surface: "Bright iu-
minary of the lonely hour, he would say,
that now sheddest thy mild and placid ray
on the woe-worm head of fortune's fugitive,
dost thou not also pensively shine on the
sacred and silent grave of my Melissa?

Favourable breezes wafted them for many days over the bosom of the Atlantic.—
At length they were overtaken by a violent
storm. The wind began to blow strongly
from the southwest, which soon increased
to a violent gale. The dirgy scud first flew
swiftly along the sky; then dark and heavy
clouds filled the atmosphere, mingling with
the top-gallant streamers of the ship. Night
hovered over the ocean, rendered horrible
by the intermitting blaze of lightnings, the
awful crash of thunder, and the deafening
roar of winds and waves. The sea was rolled
into mountains, capped with foaming fire.
Now the ship was soaring among the thunders of heaven, now sunk in the abyss of
waters.

The storm dispersed the fleet, so that
when it abated, the ship in which Alonzo
sailed was found alone; they, however, kept
on their course of destination, after repair-
ing their rigging, which had been considerably disordered by the violence of the gale.

The next morning they discovered a sail
which they fondly hoped might prove to be

one of their own fleet, and accordingly made
for it. The ship they were in pursuit of
shortened sail, and towards noon wore round
and bore down upon them, when they discovered that it was not a ship belonging to
their convoy. It appeared to be of equal
force and dimensions with that of their own;
they therefore, in order to prepare for the
worst, got ready with all speed for action.
They slowly approached each other, ma-
noeuvering for the advantage, till the strange
ship ran up British colours, and fired a gun,
which was immediately answered by the
other, under the flag of the United States.
It was not long before a close and severe
action took place, which continued for three
hours, when both ships were in so shattered
a condition that they were unable to manage a gun.* The British had lost their captain, and one half their crew, most of the
remainder being wounded.——The Americans had lost their second officer, and their
loss in men, both killed and wounded, was
nearly equal to that of the enemy.

While they lay in this condition, unable
either to annoy each other more, or to get
away, a large sail appeared, bearing down
upon them, which soon came up and proved
to be an English frigate, and which imme-

---

*The particulars of this action, in the ea ly stage of the A-
erican war, are yet remembered by many

diately took the American ship in tow, after removing the crew into the hold of the
frigate.   The crew of the British ship were
also taken on board of the frigate, which
was no sooner done than the ship went down
and was for ever buried beneath mountains
of ponderous waves.   The frigate then, with
the American ship in tow, made sail, and in
a few days reached England.   The wounded prisoners were sent to a hospital, but the
others were confined in a strong prison within the precincts of London.

The American prisoners were huddled into an apartment with British convicts of various descriptions.   Among these Alonzo
observed one whose demeanor arrested his
attention.   A deep melancholy was impressed upon his features ; his eye was wild and
despairing ; his figure was interesting, tall,
elegant and handsome.   He appeared to be
about twenty-five years of age.   He seldom
conversed, but when he did, it was readily
discovered that his education had been above
the common cast, and he possessed an en-
lightened and discriminating mind.   Alonzo
sympathetically sought his acquaintance,
and discovered therein a unison of woe.

One evening, when the prisoners were retired to rest, the stranger, upon Alonzo's
request, rehearsed the following incidents
of his life.

" You express, said he, some surprise at finding a man of my appearance in so degraded a situation; and you wish to learn the events which have plunged me in this abject state. These, when I briefly relate, your wonder will cease.

" My name is Henry Malcomb; my father was a clergyman in the west of England, and descended from one of the most respecable families in those parts. I received a classical education, and then entered the military school, as I was designed for the army, to which my earliest inclinations led. As soon as my education was considered complete, an ensign's commission was procured for me in one of the regiments destined for the West Indies. Previous to its departure for those islands, I became acquainted with a Miss Vernon, who was a few years younger than myself, and the daughter of a gentleman farmer, who had recently purchased and removed to an estate in my father's parish. Every thing that was graceful and lovely appeared centered in her person; every thing that was virtuous and excellent in her mind. I sought her hand. Our souls soon became united by the indissoluble bonds of sincerest love, and as there were no parental or other impediments to our union, it was agreed that as soon as I returned from the Indies, where it was expected that my stay would be short, the marriage solemnities should be performed. Solemn oaths of constancy passed between us, and I sailed, with my regiment, for the Indies.

" While there, I received from her, and returned letters filled with the tenderest expressions of anxiety and regret of absence. At length the time came when we were to embark for England, where we arrived after an absence of about eighteen months. The moment I got on land I hastened to the house of Mr. Vernon, to see the charmer of my soul. She received me with all the ardency of affection, and even shed tears of joy in my presence. I pressed her to name the day which was to perfect our union and happiness, and the next Sunday, four days only distant, was agreed upon for me to lead her to the altar. How did my heart bound at the prospect of making Miss Vernon my own !—of possessing in her all that could render life agreeable; I hastened home to my family and informed them of my approaching bliss, who all sympathized in the anticipated joy which swelled my bosom.

" I had a sister some years older than myself, who had been the friend and inmate of my angel in my absence. They were now almost every day together, so that I had frequent opportunities of her company.

one day she had been with my sister at my father's, and I attended her home. On my return, my sister requested me to attend her in a private room. We therefore retired, and when we were seated she thus addressed me

Henry, you know that to promote your peace, your welfare, and your happiness, has ever been the pride of my heart. Nothing except this could extort the secret which I shall now disclose, and which has yet remained deposited in my own bosom: my duty to a brother whom I esteem dear as life, forbids me to remain silent. As an affectionate sister, I cannot tacitly see you thus imposed upon; I cannot see you the dupe and slave of an artful and insidious woman, who does not sincerely return your love, nor can I bear to see your marriage consummated with one whose soul and affections are placed upon another object."

"Here she hesitated—while I, with insufferable anguish of mind, begged her to proceed.

"About six or eight months after your departure, she continued, it was reported to Miss Vernon that she had a rival in the Indies; that you had there found an American beauty, on whom you lavished those endearments which belonged of right to her alone. This news made, at first, a deep

14

impression on her mind, but it soon wore away; and whether from this cause, from fickleness of disposition, or that she never sincerely loved you, I know not; but this I do know, that a youth has been for some time past her almost constant companion. To convince you of this, you need only to-morrow evening, about sunset, conceal your-self near the long avenue by the side of the rivulet, back of Mr. Vernon's country-house, where you will undoubtedly surprise Miss Vernon and her companion ·in their usual evening's walk. If I should be mistaken I will submit to your censure; but should you find it as I have predicted, you have only to rush from your concealment, charge her with her perfidy, and renounce her forever."

"Of all the plagues, of all the torments, of all the curses which torture the soul, jealousy of arival in love is the worst. Enraged, confounded and astonished, it seemed as if my bosom would have instantaneously burst. To conceal my emotions, I left my sister's apartment, after having thanked her for her information, and proceeded to obey her injunctions. I retired to my own room, and there poured out my execrations.

"Cursed woman! I exclaimed, is it thus you requite my tender love! Could a vague report of my inconstancy drive you to infidelity' Did not my continual letters breathe constant adoration? And did not yours portray the same sincerity of affection? No, it was not that which caused you to perjure your plighted vows. It was that damnable passion for novelty, which more or less holds a predominancy over your whole sex. To a new coat, a new face, a new rover, you will sacrifice honour, principle and virtue. And to those, backed by splendid power and splendid property, you will forfeit your most sacred engagements, though made in the presence of heaven.—Thus did I rave through a sleepless night.

"The next day I walked into the fields, and before the time my sister appointed had arrived, I had worked up my feelings almost to the frenzy of distraction. I repaired, however, to the spot, and concealed myself in the place she had named, which was a tuft of laurels by the side of the walk. I soon perceived Miss Vernon strolling down the avenue, arm in arm with a young man elegantly dressed, and of singular, delicate appearance. They were earnestly conversing in a low tone of voice; the hand of my false fair one was gently pressed in the hand of the stranger. As soon as they had passed the place of my concealment, they turned aside and seated themselves in a little arbour, a few yards distant from where I sat. The stranger clasped Miss Vernon

in his arms : " Dearest angel ' he exclaimed, what an interruption to our bliss by the
return of my hated rival !" With fond ca-
resses and endearing blandishments, " fear
nothing, she replied ; I have promised and
must yield him my hand, but you shall never be excluded from my heart ; we shall
find sufficient opportunities for private con-
ference." I could contain myself no longer
—my brain was on fire.   Quick as lightning I sprang from my covert, and presenting a pistol which I had concealed under my
robe,—" Die ! said I, thou false and perjur-
ed wretch, by the hand thou hast dishonour-
ed, a death too mild for so foul a crime !"
and immediately shot Miss Vernon through
the head, who fell lifeless at my feet ! Then
suddenly drawing my sword, "And thou,
perfidious contaminator and destroyer of
my bliss ! cried I—go ! attend thy companion in iniquity to the black regions of ever-
lasting torment !" So saying, I plunged my
sword into his bosom. A screech of agony,
attended by the exclamation, " *Henry, your
wife ! your sister* !" awoke me, too late, to
terrors unutterable, to anguish unspeakable,
to woes irretrievable, and insupportable despair! It was indeed my betrothed wife, it was
indeed my affectionate sister, arrayed in
man's habit. The one lay dead before me, the
other weltering in her blood ! With a feeble

and expiring voice, my sister informed me, that in a gay and inconsiderate moment they had concerted this plan, to try my jealousy, determining to discover themselves as soon as they had made the experiment. "I forgive you, Henry, she said, I forgive your mistake," and closed her eyes for ever in death! What a scene for sensibilities like mine! To paint or describe it, exceeds the power of language or imagination. I instantly turned the sword against my own bosom; an unknown hand arrested it, and prevented its entering my heart. The report of the pistol, and the dying screech of my sister, had alarmed Mr. Vernon's family, who arrived at that moment, one of whom had seized my arm, and thus hindered me from destroying my own life. I submitted to be bound and conveyed to prison. My trial came on at the last assizes. I made no defence; and was condemned to death. My execution will take place in eight weeks from to-morrow. I shall cheerfully meet my fate; for who would endure life when rendered so peculiarly miserable!"

The wretched Malcomb here ended his tale of woe. No tear moistened his eye—his grief was too despairing for tears; it preyed upon his heart, drank the vital streams of life, and burst in convulsive sighs from his burning bosom.   K

14 *

Alonzo seriously contemplated on the in
cidents and events of this tragical story.
Conscience whispered him, are not Malcomb's miseries superior to thine ? Candour
and correct reason must have answered yes
" Melissa perished, said Alonzo, but not by
the hand of her lover : she expired, but not
through the mistaken frenzy of him who
adored her. She died, conscious of the un-
feigned love I bore her."

Alonzo and his fellow prisoners had been
robbed, when they were captured, of every
thing except the clothes they wore.   Their
allowance of provisions was scanty and poor.
They were confined in the third story of a
lofty prison.   Time rolled away ; no prospects appeared of their liberation, either by
exchange or parole.   Some of the prisoners
were removed, as new ones were introduced, to other places of confinement, until not
one American was left except Alonzo.

Meantime the day appointed for the execution of Malcomb drew near.   His past
and approaching fate filled the breast of A-
lonzo with sympathetic sorrow.   He saw
his venerable father, his mother, his friends
and acquaintance, with several pious cler-
gymen, frequently enter the prison to console and comfort him, and to prepare him
for the unchangeable state on which he was
soon to enter.   He saw his mind softened

by their advice and counsel;—frequntly
would he burst into tears;—often in the solitary hours of night was he heard addressing.
the throne of grace for mercy and forgiv-
ness.   But the grief that preyed at his heart
had wasted him to a mere skeleton; a slow
but deleterious fever had consequently im-
planted itself in his constitution.   Exhausted nature could make but a weak struggle
against disease and affliction like his, and
about a week previous to the day appointed
for his execution, he expired in peace and
penitence, trusting in the mercy of his Creator through the sufferings of a Redcemer.
   Soon after this event, orders came for removing some of the prisoners to a most
loathsome place of coufinement in the sub-
urbs of the city.   It fell to Alonzo's lot to
be one.   He therefore formed a project for
escaping.   He had observed that the gratings in one of the windows of the apartment
were loose and could be easily removed.
One night, when the prisoners were asleep
he stripped off his clothes, every article of
which he cut into narrow strips, tied them
together, fastened one end to one of the
strongest gratings, removed the others until
he had made on opening large enough to get
out, and then, by the rope he had made of
his clothes, let himself down into the yard
of the prison.   There he found a   long

piece of timber, which he dragged to the wall, clambered up thereon, and sprang over into the street. His shoes and hat he had left in the prison, as a useless encumbrance without his clothes, all which he had converted into the means of escape, so that he was now literally stark naked. He stood a moment to reflect :—" Here am I, said he, freed from my local prison indeed, but in the midst of an enemy's country, without a friend, without the means of obtaining one day's subsistence, surrounded by the darkness of night, destitute of a single article of clothing, and even unable to form a resolution what step next to take. The ways of heaven are marvellous—may I silently bow to its dispensations!"

Alonzo passed along the street in this forlorn condition, not knowing where to proceed, or what course to take. It was about three o'clock in the morning, the street was illuminated by lamps, and he feared falling into the hands of the watch. For some time he saw no person ; at length a voice from the other side of the street called out,——Hallo, messmate! what, scudding under bare poles ? You must have experienced a severe gale indeed thus to have carried away every rag of sail!"

Alonzo turned, and saw the person who spoke. He was a decent looking man, of

middle age, dressed in a sailor'shabit. A-
lonzo had often heard of the generosity and
honourable conduct of the British tars : he
therefore approached him and told him his
real case, not even concealing his being taken in actual hostility to the British gov-
ernment, and his escape from prison. The
sailor mused a few minutes. "Thy case
said he, is a little critical, but do not despair. Had I met thee as an enemy, I
should have fought thee; but as it is, com-
passion is the first consideration. Perhaps
I may be in as bad a situation before the
war is ended." Then slipping off his coat
and giving it to Alonzo, "follow me," he
said, and turning, walked hastily along the
street, followed by Alonzo; he passed into
a bye-lane, entered a small house, and taking Alonzo into a back room, opened a
trunk, and handed out a shirt: "there, said
he, pointing to a bed, you can sleep till
morning, when we will see what can be done.'

The next morning the sailor brought in a
very decent suit of clothes and presented
them to Alonzo. "You will make this
place your home, said he, until more favor-
able prospects appear. In this great city
you will be safe, for even your late gaoler
would not recognize you in this dress. And
perhaps some opportunity may offer by
which you may return to your own country"

He told Alonzo that his name was Jack Brown; that he was a midshipman on board the Severn; that he had a wife and four children, and owned the house in which they then were. " In order to prevent sus- picion or discovery, said he, I shall consid- er you as a relation from the country until you are better provided for." Alonzo was then introduced to the sailor's wife, an a- miable woman, and here he remained for several weeks.

One day Alonzo was informed that a number of American prisoners were brought in. He went to the place where they were landed, and saw several led away to prison, and some who were sick or disabled, car- ried to the hospital. As the hospital was near at hand, Alonzo entered it to see how the sick and disabled prisoners were treated.

He found that they received as much attention as could reasonably be expect- ed.* As he passed along the different a- partments he was surprised at hearing his name called by a faint voice. He turned to the place from whence it proceeded, and saw stretched on a mattress, a person who appeared on the point of expiring. His vi-

_____

*The Americans who were imprisoned in England, in the time of war, were treated with much more humanity than those who were imprisoned in America.

sage was pale and emaciated, his countenance haggard and ghastly, his eyes inexpressive and glazy. He held out his withered hand, and feebly beckoned to Alonzo, who immediately approached him. His features appeared not unfamiliar to Alonzo, but for a moment he could not recollect him. "You do not know me," said the apparently dying stranger. 'Beauman!" exclaimed Alonzo, in surprise. "Yes, replied the sick man, it is Beauman; you behold me on the verge of eternity; I have but a short time to continue in this world." Alonzo enquired how he came in the power of the enemy. "By the fate of wa, he replied; I was taken in an action on York Island, carried on board a prison-ship in New-York, and sent with a number of others for England. I had received a wound in my thigh, from a musket ball, during the action; the wound mortified, and my thigh was amputated on the voyage; since which I have been rapidly wasting away, and I now feel that the cold hand of death is laid upon me." Here he became exhausted, and for some time remained silent. Alonzo had not before discovered that he had lost his leg: he now found that it had been taken off close to his body, and that he was worn to skeleton. When Beauman revived, he enquired into Alonzo's affairs. Alonzo related all that had happened to him after leaving New London.

"You are unhappy, Alonzo, said Beauman, in the death of your Melissa, to which it is possible I have been, undesignedly accessory. I could say much on the subject, would my strength permit; but it is needless. She is gone, and I must soon go also. She was sent to her uncle's at Charleston, by her father, where I was soon to follow her. It was supposed that thus widely removed from all access to your company, she would yield to the persuasion of her friends to renounce you: her unexpected death, however, frustrated every design of this nature, and overwhelmed her father and family in inexpressible woe."

Here Beauman ceased. Alonzo found he wanted rest: he enquired whether he was in want of any thing to render him more comfortable. Beauman replied that he was not: "For the comforts of this life, said he, I have no relish; medical aid is applied, but without effect." Alonzo then left him, promising to call again in the morning.

When Alonzo called the next morning, he perceived an alarming alteration in Beauman. His extremities were cold, a chilling, clammy sweat stood upon his face, his respiration was short and interrupted, his

pulse weak and intermitting.	He took the
hand of Alonzo, and feebly pressing it,—"I
am dying, said he in a faint voice.	If ever
you return to America, inform my friends
of my fate."	This Alonzo readily enga-
ged to do, and told him also that he would
not leave him.

Becuman soon fell into a stupor; sensation became suspended; his eyes rolled up
and fixed.	Sometimes a partial revival
would take place, when he would fall into
incoherent muttering, calling on the names
of his deceased father, his mother and Melissa; his voice dying away in imperfect
moanings, till his lips continued to move
without sound.	Towards night he lay si-
lent, and only continued to breathe with
difficulty, till a slight convulsion gave the
freed spirit to the unknown regions of im-
material existence.	Alonzo followed his
remains to the grave : a natural stone was
placed at its head, on which Alonzo, unob-
served, carved the initials of the deceased's name, with the date of his death, and
left him to moulder with his native dust.

A few days after this event, Jack Brown
informed Alonzo that he had procured the
means of his escape.	A person with whom
I am acquainted, said he, and whom I suppose to be a smuggler, has agreed to carry
you to France.	There, by application to

the American minister, you will be enabled
to get to your own country, if that is your
object. About midnight I will pilot you on
board, and by to-morrow's sun you may be
in France."

At the time appointed, Jack set out,
bearing a large trunk on his shoulder, and
directed Alonzo to follow him. They proceeded down to a quay, and went on board
a small skiff. " Here, said Jack to the captain, is the gentleman I spoke to you a-
bout," and delivered him the trunk. Then
taking Alonzo aside, " in that trunk, said
he, are a few changes of linen, and here is
something to help you till you can help
yourself." So saying, he slipped ten guineas into his hand. Alonzo expressed his
gratitude with tears. " Say nothing, said
Jack, we were born to help each other in
distress, and may Jack never weather a
storm or splice a rope, if he permits a fellow creature to suffer with want while he
has a luncheon on board." He then shook
Alonzo by the hand, wishing him a good
voyage, and went whistling away. The
skiff soon sailed, and the next morning A-
lonzo was landed in France. Alonzo proceeded immediately to Paris, not with a
view of returning to America; he had yet
no relish for revisiting the land of his sorrows, the scenes where at every step his

heart must bleed afresh, though to bleed it had never ceased. But he was friendless in a strange land : perhaps, through the aid of the American minister, Dr. Franklin, to whose fame Alonzo was no stranger, he might be placed in a situation to procure bread, which was all he at present hoped or wished.

. He therefore presented himself before the doctor, whom he found in his study.— To be informed that he was an American and unfortunate, was sufficient to arouse the feelings of Franklin. He desired Alonzo to be seated, and to recite his history. This he readily complied with, not concealing his attachment to Melissa, her father's barbarity, her death in consequence, his own father's failure, with all the particulars of his leaving America, his capture, escape from prison, and arrival in France ; as also the town of his nativity, the name of his father, and the particular circumstances of his family ; concluding by expressing his unconquerable reluctance to return to his native country, which now would be to him only a gloomy wilderness, and that his present object was only some means of support.

The doctor enquired of Alonzo the particular circumstances and time of his father's failure. Of this Alonzo gave him a minute account. Franklin then sat in deep

contemplation for the space of fifteen min-
ates, without speaking a word.   He then
took his pen, wrote a short note, directed
t, and gave it to Alonzo : " Deliver this,
said he, to the person to whom it is directed ; he will find you employment, until
something mo•? favourable may offer.''
    Alonzo took the note, thanked the doc-
tor, and went in search of the person to
whom it was addressed.   He soon found
the house, which was situated in one of the
most popular streets in Paris.   He knocked at the door, which was opened by an
elderly looking man : Alonzo enquired for
the name to whom the note was addressed.
The gentleman informed him that he was
the man.   Alonzo presented him the note,
which having read, he desired him to walk
in, and ordered supper.   After supper he
informed Alonzo that he was an English
bookseller ; that he should employ him as
a clerk, and desired to know what wages he
demanded. . Alonzo replied that he should
submit that to him, being unacquainted with
the customary salary of clerks in that line
of business.   The gentleman told him that
the matter should be arranged the next day.
His name was Grafton.
    The next morning Mr. Grafton took A-
lonzo into his bookstore, and gave him his
instructions.   His business was to sell the

books to customers, and a list of prices was given him for that purpose. Mr. Grafton counted out twenty crowns and gave them to Alonzo : " You may want some necessaries, said he ; and as you have set no price on your services, we shall not differ about the wages if you are attentive and faithful."

Alonzo gave his employer no room to complain; nor had he any reason to be discontented with his situation. Mr. Grafton regularly advanced him twenty crowns at the commencement of every month, and boarded him in his family. Alonzo dressed himself in deep mourning. He sought no company ; he found consolation only in solitude, if consolation it could be called.

As he was walking out early one morning, he discovered something lying in the street, which he at first supposed to be a small piece of silk : he took it up and found it to be a curiously wrought purse, containing a few guineas with some small pieces of silver, and something at the bottom carefully wrapped in a piece of paper; he unfolded it, and was thunderstruck at beholding an elegant miniature of Melissa ! Her sweetly pensive features, her expressive countenance, her soul-enlivening eye ! The shock was almost too powerful for his senses. Wildered in a maze of wonders, he knew not what to conjecture. Melissa's

15 *

miniature found in the streets of Paris, af-
er she had some time been dead! He
riewed it, he clasped it to his bosom.—
" Such, said he, did she appear, ere the cor-
roding cankers of grief had blighted he*
heavenly charms! By what providential
miracle am I possessed of the likeness,
when the original is no more? What benevo-
'ent angel has taken pity on my sufferings,
nd conveyed to me this inestimable prize?"

But though he had thus become possessed of what he esteemed most valuable,
what right had he to withhold it from the
lawful owner, could the owner indeed be
found? Perhaps the person who had lost
it would part with it; perhaps the money
contained in the purse was of more value
to that person than the miniature. At any
rate, justice required that he should endeavour to find to whom it belonged : this he
might do by advertising, which he immediately concluded upon, resolving, should the
owner appear, to purchase the miniature,
_? possibly within his power.

Passing into another street, he saw several
hand-bills stuck up on the walls of houses '
stepping up to one, he read as follows :

" Lost, between the hours of nine and
ten last evening, in the *Rue de Loir*, a small
silk purse, containing a few pieces of money,
and a lady's miniature. One hundred

crowns will be given to the person who may have found it, and will restore it to the owner at the *American Hotel*, near the *Louvre*, Room No. 4. "

It was printed both in the French and English languages. By the reward here offered, Alonzo was convinced that the miniature belonged to some person who set a value upon it. Determined to explicate the mystery, he proceeded immediately to the place, found the room mentioned in the bill, and knocked at the door. A servant appeared, of whom Alonzo enquired for the lodger. The servant answered him in French, which Alonzo did not understand : he replied in his own language, but found it was unintelligible to the servant. A grave middle aged gentleman then came to the door from within the room and ended their jabbering at each other: he, in the English language, desired Alonzo to walk in. It was an apartment neatly furnished; no person was therin except the gentleman and servant before mentioned, and a person who sat writing in a corner of the room, with his back towards them.

Alonzo informed the gentleman that he had called according to the direction in a bill of advertisement to enquire for the person who the preceding night, had lost a purse and miniature. The person who was

writing had hitherto taken no notice of
what had passed; but at the sound of A-
lonzo's voice, after he had entered the
room, he started and turned about, and at
mention of the miniature, he rose up. A-
lonzo fixed his eyes upon him: they both
stood for a few moments silent: for a short
time their recollection was confused and
imperfect, but the mists of doubt were soon
dissipated. "Edgar!"—"Alonzo!" they
alternately exclaimed. It was indeed Edgar, the early friend and fellow student of
Alonzo—the brother of Melissa! In an instant they were in each others arms.

Edgar and Alonzo retired to a separate
room. Edgar informed Alonzo that the
news of Melissa's death reached him, by a
letter from his father, while with the army;
that he immediately procured a furlough,
and visited his father, whom, with his mother, he found in inconsolable distress.—"The
letter which my uncle had written, said Edgar, announcing her death, mentioned with
what patience and placidity she endured her
malady, and with what calmness and resignation she met the approach of death. Her
last moments, like her whole life, were un-
ruffled and serene. She is in heaven Alonzo—she is an angel'"—Swelling grief here'
choaked the utterance of Edgar; for some

time he could proceed no farther, and Alonzo, with bursting bosom, mingled his tears.

"My father, resumed Edgar, bent on
uniting her to Beauman or at least of prevent-
ing her union with you, had removed her
to a desolate family mansion, and placed
her under the care of an aunt. At that
place, he either suspected, on really discovered that you had recourse to her while my
aunt was absent on business. She was therefore no longer entrusted to the care of her
aunt, but my father immediately formed and
executed the plan of sending her to his
brother in South Caroiina, under pretence
of restoring her to health by change of climate, as her health in reality had began
rapidly to decay. There it was designed
that Beauman should shortly follow her,
with recommendations from my father to
her uncle, urging him to use all possible
means which might tend to persuade her to
become the wife of Beauman. But change
of climate only encreased the load of sorrows, and she soon sunk beneath them.
The letter mentioned nothing of her troubles: possibly my uncle's family knew
nothing of them : to them, probably,

———"She never told her love,
But sat like Patience on a monument
Smiling at grief; while sad concealment,
Like a worm in the bud,
Fed on her damask cheek.		L

" My father's distress was excessive : of ten did he accuse himself of barbarity, and he once earnestly expressed a wish that he had consented to her union with you.   My father, I know, is parsimonious, but he sincerely loved his children.   Inflexible as is his nature, the untimely death of a truly affectionate and only daughter will, I much fear, precipitate him, and perhaps my mother also, to a speedy grave.

"As soon as my feelings would permit, I repaired to your father's, and made enquiry concerning you.   I found your parents content in their humble state, except that your father had been ill, but was recovering.   Of you they had heard nothing since your departure, and they deeply lamented your absence.   And from Vincent I could obtain no farther information.

Sick of the world, I returned to the army.   An American consul was soon to sail for Holland :—I solicited and obtained the appointment of secretary.   I hoped by visiting distant countries, in some measure to relieve my mind from the deep melancholy with which it was oppressed.   We were to proceed first to Paris, where we have been a few days; to-morrow we are to depart for Holland.   The consul is the man who introduced you into the room where you found me.

"Last evening I lost the miniature which I suppose you have found: the chain to which it was suspended around my neck, had broken while I was walking the street I carefully wrapped it in paper and deposit ed it in my purse, which I probably drop. ped on replacing it in my pocket, and did not discover the loss until this morning. I immediately made diligent search, but not finding it, I put up bills of advertisement. The likeness was taken in my sister's happiest days. After I had entered upon my professional studies in New-York, I became acquainted with a miniature painter, who took my likeness. He afterwards went into the country, and as I found he was to pass near my father's, I engaged him to call there and take my sister's likeness also. We exchanged them soon after. It was dear to me, even while the original remained; but since she is gone it has become a most precious and valuable relique."

All the tender powers of Alonzo's soul were called into action by Edgar's recital. The " days of other years"—the ghosts of sepulchered blessings, passed in painful review. Added to these, the penurious condition of his parents, his father's recent illness. and his probable inability to procure the bread of his family, all tended more deeply to sink his spirits in the gulf of mel

ancholy and misery. He however informed
Edgar of all that had hapened since they
parted at Vincent's—respecting the old mansion Melissa's extraordinary disappearance
therefrom, the manner in which he was informed of her death, his departure from A-
meica, capture, escape, Beauman's death,
arrival in France, and his finding the miniature. To Edgar as well as Alonzo, Melissa sudden and unaccountable removal
from the mansion was mysterious and inexplicable.

As Edgar was to depart early the next
morning, they neither slept nor separated
that night.

"If it were not for your reluctance to re-
visit your native country, said Edgar, I
should urge you to accompany me to Holland, and thence return with me to America. Necessity and duty require that I
should not be long absent, as my parents want
my assistance, and they are now childless."

"Suffer me, answered Alonzo, to bury
myself in this city for the present : should
I ever again awake to real life, I will seek
you out if you are on the earth ;—but now,
I can only be a companion to my miseries."

The next morning as they were about to
depart, Alonzo took Melissa's miniature
from his bosom, contemplated the picture
a few moments with ardent emotion, and

presented it to Edgar. " Keep it, said Edgar, it is thine. I bestow it upon thee as I would the original, had not death become the rival of thy love, and my affection.— Suffer not the sacred symbol too tenderly to renew your sorrows. How swiftly, Alonzo, does this restless life fleet away!— How soon shall we pass the barriers of terrestrial existence! Let us live worthy of ourselves, of our holy religion, of Melissa— Melissa, whom, when a few more suns have arisen and set, we shall meet in regions where all tears shall be eternally wiped from every eye."

With what unspeakable sensibilities was it returned to Alonzo's bosom! Edgar offered Alonzo pecuniary assistance, which the latter refused: " I am in business, said he, which brings me a decent support, and that is sufficient." They agreed to write each other as frequently as possible, and then affectionately parted: Edgar sailed for Holland, and Alonzo returned to his business at Mr. Grafton's.

Some time after this Alonzo received a message from Dr. Franklin, requiring his attendance at his house, which summons he immediately obeyed. The doctor introduced him into his study, and after being seated, he earnestly viewed Alonzo for some time, and thus addressed him :

16

" Young man, your views, your resolutions, and your present conduct, are totally wrong. Disappointment, you say, has driven you from your native country. Disappointment in what? In obtaining the object on which you most doated. And suppose this object had been obtained, would your happiness have been complete? Your own reason, if you coolly consult it, will convince you of the contrary. Do you not remember when an infant, how you cried, and teazed your nurse, or your parents, for a rattle, or some gay trinket?—Your whole soul was fixed upon the enchanting bauble; but when obtained, you soon cast it away, and sighed as earnestly for some other trifle, some new toy. Thus it is through life; the fancied value of an object ceases with the attainment; it becomes familiar, and its charm is lost.

" Was it the splendours of beauty which enraptured you? Sickness may, and age must destroy the symmetry of the most finished form—the brilliancy of the finest features. Was it the graces of the mind? I tell you, that by familiarity, these allurements are lost, and the mind, left vacant, turns to some other source to supply vaeuun.

" Stripped of all their intrinsic value, how poor how vain, and how worthless, are those things we name pleasures, and enjoyments

" Besides, the attainment of your wishes might have been the death of your hopes. If my reasoning is correct, the ardency of your passion might have closed with the pursuit. An every day suit, however rich and costly the texture, is soon worn threadbare. On your part, indifference would consequently succeed : on the part of your partner, disappointment, jealousy, and disgust. What might follow is needless for me to name ;—your soul must shudder at the idea of conjugal infidelity !

" But admitting the most favourable consequences ; turn the brightest side of the picture ; admitting as much happiness as the connubial state will allow : how might your bosom have been wounded by the sickness and death of your children, or their disorderly and disobedient conduct ! You must know also, that the warmth of youthful passion must soon cease, and it is merely a hazardous chance whether friendship will supply the absence of affection.

"After all, my young friend, it will be well for you to consider, whether the allwise dispensing hand of Providence, has not directed this matter which you esteem so great an affliction, for your greatest good, and most essential advantage. And suffer me to tell you, that in all my observations on life, I have always found that those connections which were formed from inordinate passion, or what some would call pure affection, have been ever the most unhappy. Examine the varied circles of society, you will there see this axiom demonstrated; you will there see how few among the sentimentally refined are even apparently at ease; while those, insusceptible of what you name tender attachments, or who receive them only as things of course, plod on through life, without even experiencing the least inconvenience from a want of the pleasures they are *supposed* to bestow, or the pains they are sure to create. Beware, then, my son, beware of yielding the heart to the effeminacies of passion. Exquisite sensibilities are ever subject to exquisite inquietudes. Counsel with correct reason, place entire dependence on the SUPREME, and the triumph of fortitude and resignation will be yours."

Franklin paused. His reasonings, however they convinced the understanding, could not heal the wounds of Alonzo's bosom.—In Melissa he looked for as much happiness as earth could afford, nor could he see any prospect in life which could repair the loss he had sustained.

" You have, resumed the philosopher, deserted an indulgent father, a fond and tender mother, who must want your aid; now,

perhaps, unable to toil for bread ; now, pos
sibly laid upon the bed of sickness, calling,
in anguish or delirium, for the filial hand of
their only son to administer relief."——All
the parental feelings of Alonzo were now
called into poignant action.——" You have
left a country, bleeding at every pore, des-
olated by the ravages of war, wrecked by
· the thunders of battle, her heroes slain, her
children captured. This country asks—she
demands—you owe her your services : God
and nature call upon you to defend her,
while here you bury yourself in inglorious
inactivity, pining for a hapless object, which,
by all your lamentations, you can never
bring back to the regions of mortality."

This aroused the patriotic flame in the
bosom o. Alonzo, and he voluntarily exclaimed, " I will go to the relief of my parents—I will fly to the defence of my country !"

"In former days, continued Franklin, I
was well acquainted with your father. As
soon as you informed me of his failure, I
wrote to my correspondent in England, and
found, as I expected, that he had been over-
reached by swindlers and sharpers.——The
pretended failure of the merchants with
whom he was in company, was all a sham,
as, also the reported loss of the ships in their
employ. The merchants fled to England :

16 *

I have had them arrested, and they have given up their effects to much more than the amount of their debts. I have therefore procured a reversion of your father's losses, which, with costs, damages, and interests, when legally stated, he will receive of my agent in Philadelphia, to whom I shall transmit sufficient documents by you, and I shall advance you a sum equal to the expenses of your voyage, which will be liquidated by the said agent. A ship sails in a few days from Havre, for Savannah in Georgia: it would, indeed, be more convenient were she bound to some more northern port, but I know of no other which will sail for any part of America for some time. In her therefore I would advise you to take passage: it is not very material on what part of the continent you are landed; you will soon reach Philadelphia, transact your business, restore your father to his property, and be ready to serve your country."

If any thing could have given Alonzo consolation, it must have been this noble, generous and disinterested conduct of the great Franklin in favour of his father, by which his family were restored to ease and to independence. Ah! had this but have happened in time to save a life far dearer than his own! The reflection was too painful. The idea, however, of giving joy to his aged

parents, hastened his departure. Furnished
with proper documents and credentials from
Franklin, his benefactor, he took leave of
him, with the warmest expressions of gratitude, as also of Mr. Grafton, and sailed for
Savannah, where he arrived in about eight
weeks.

Intent on his purpose, he immediately
purchased a carriage and proceeded on for
Philadelphia. As he approached Charleston, his bosom swelled with mournful recol-
lections. He arrived in that city in the afternoon, and at evening he walked out, and
entered a little ale house, which stood near
the large burial ground. An elderly woman
and two small children were the only persons in the house, except himself. After
calling for a pint of ale, he enquired of the
old lady, if Col D——, (Melissa's uncle)
did not live near the city. She informed
him that he resided about a mile from the
town, where he had an elegant seat, and
that he was very rich.

"Was there not a young lady, asked A-
lonzo, who died there about eighteen
months ago?"

"La me! said she, did you know her?
Yes: and a sweeter or more handsome lady the sun never shined on. And then she
was so good, so patient in her sickness.—
Poer, dear distressed girl, she pined away

to skin and bones before she died. She
was not Col. D——'s daughter, only somehow related: she came here in hopes that
a change of air might do her good. She
came from—la me! I cannot think of the
name of the place; it is a crabbed name
though."

"Connecticut, was it not?" said Alonzo.

"O yes, that was it, replied she. Dear
me! then you knew her, did you, sir?—
Well, we have not her like left in Charleston, that we han't;—and then there was
such ado at her funeral; five hundred people, I dare say, with eight young ladies for
pall-bearers, all dressed in white, with black
ribbons, and all the bells tolling."

"Where was she buried?" enquired A-
lonzo.

"In the church-yard right before our
door, she answered. My husband is the
sexton; he put up her large white marble
tomb-stones;——they are the largest and
whitest in the whole burying-ground; and
so, indeed, they ought to be, for never was
there a person who deserved them more."

Tired with the old woman's garrulity,
and with a bosom bursting with anguish,
Alonzo paid for his ale without drinking it,
bade her good night, and slowly proceeded
to the church-yard. The moon, in full lustre, shone with solemn, silvery ray, on the

sacred piles, and funeral monuments of the
sacred dead; the wind murmured mournfully among the weeping willows; a solitary nightingale* sang plaintively in the distant forest; and a whippoorwill, Melissa's
favourite bird, whistled near the portico of
the church.   The large white tomb-stones
soon caught the eye of Alonzo.   He approached them with tremulous step, and
with feelings too agitated for description.
On the head-stone he read as follows:
SACRED
To the Memory of inestimable departed
WORTH;
To unrivalled Excellence and Virtue.
Miss MELISSA D———,
Whose remains are deposited here, and
whose ethereal part became a seraph,
October 26, 1776,
In the 18th year of her age.
Alonzo bent, kneeled, he prostrated himself, he clasped the green turf which enclosed her grave, he watered it with his tears,
he warmed it with his sighs.   "Where art
thou, bright beam of heavenly light! he
said.   Come to my troubled soul, blessed
spirit!   Come, holy shade!   come in all
thy native loveliness, and cheer the bosom

---

*This bird, though not an inhabitant of the northern states, is
frequently to be met with in Georgia and the Carolinas.

of wretchedness, by thy grief dispersing smile! On the ray of yon evening star descend. One moment leave the celestial regions of glory—leave, one moment, thy sister beatitudes, and glide, in entrancing beauty, before me: wave, benignly wave thy white hand, and assuage the anguish of despairing sorrow! Alas! in vain my invocation! A curtain, impenetrable, is drawn betwixt me and thee, only to be disclosed by the dissolution of nature."

He arose and walked away: suddenly he stopped. "Yet, said he, if spirits departed lose not the power of recollection;—if they have knowledge of present events on earth, Melissa cannot have forgotten me—she must pity me." He returned to the grave; he took her miniature from his bosom; he held it up, and earnestly viewed it by the moon's pale ray.

"Ah, Franklin! he exclaimed, how tenderly does she beam her lovely eye upon me! How often have I drank delicious extacy from the delicacy of those unrivalled charms! How often have they taught me to anticipate superlative and uninterrupted bliss! Mistaken and delusive hope! [*returning the miniature to his bosom.*] Vain and presumptuous assurance. Then [*pointing to the grave*] there behold how my dearest wishes, my fondest expectations are realized !——Hallowed turf! lie lightly on her bosom !—Sacred willows ! sprinkle the dews gently over her grave, while the mourning breezes sigh sadly amid your branches! Here may the "widowed wild rose love to bloom!" Here may the first placid beams of morning delight to linger ; from hence, the evening ray reluctantly withdraw!— And when the final trump shall renovate and arouse the sleeping saint;—when on "buoyant step" she soars to glory, may our meeting spirits join in beatifick transport! May my enraptured ear catch the first holy whisper of her consecrated lips."

Alonzo having thus poured out the effusions of an overcharged heart, pensively returned to the inn, which he entered and seated himself in the common room, in deep contemplation. As usual at public inns, a number of people were in the room, among whom were several officers of the American army. Alonzo was too deeply absorbed in melancholy reflection, to notice passing incidents, until a young officer came, seated himself by him, and entered into conversation respecting the events of the war. He appeared to be about Alonzo's age; his person was interesting, his manners sprightly, his observations correct.— Alonzo was, in some degree, aroused from his abstractedness;—the manners of the stranger pleased him. His frankness, his ease, his understanding, his urbanity, void of vanity or sophistication, sympathetically caught the feelings of Alonzo, and he even felt a sort of solemn regret when the stranger departed. He soon retired to bed, determining to proceed early in the morning.

He arose about daylight; the horizon was overcast, and it had begun to rain, which before sunrise had encreased to a violent storm. He found therefore that he must content himself to stay until it was over, which did not happen till near night, and too late to pursue his journey. He wa informed by the inn-keeper, that the theatre, which had been closed since the commencement of the war, was to be opened that night only, with the tragedy of *Gustavus*, and close with a representation of Burgoyne's capture, and some other recent events of the American war. To "wing the hours with swifter speed," Alonzo determined to go to the theatre, and at the hour appointed he repaired thither.

As he was proceeding to take his seat, he passed the box where sat the young officer, whose manners had so prepossessed him the preceding evening at the inn. He immediately arose: they exchanged salutations, and Alonzo walked on and took his seat. The evening was warm, and the house exceedingly crowded. After the tragedy was through, and before the after-piece commenced, the young officer came to Alonzo's box, and made some remarks on the merit of the actors. While they were discoursing, a bustle took place in one part of the house, and several people gathered around a box, at a little distance from them. The officer turned, left Alonzo, and hastened to the place. To the general enquiry, *"what's the matter?"* it was answered, that "a lady had fainted." She was led out, and the tumult subsided.

As soon as the after-piece was closed, Alonzo returned to the inn. As he passed along he cast his eyes toward the churchyard, where lay the " wither'd blessings of his richest joys." Affection, passion, inclination, urged him to go and breathe a farewell sigh, to drop a final tear over the grave of Melissa. Discretion, reason, wisdom forbade it—forbade that he re-pierce the ten thousand wounds of his bosom, by the acute revival of unavailing sorrows He hurried to his chamber.

As he prepared to retire to rest, he saw a book lying on the table near his bed. On taking it up he found it to be *Young's Night Thoughts*, a book which, in happier days, had been the solace of many a gloomy, many a lucid hour. He took it up and the

17 M

first lines he cast his eyes upon were the following :

> " Song, beauty, youth, love, virtue, joy: this group
> Of bright ideas—flowers of Paradise,
> As yet unforfeit! in one blaze we bind.
> Kneel, and present it to the skies ; as all
> We guess of Heaven! And *these* were all her own
> And she was mine, and I was—was most blest—
> Like blossom'd trees o'erturn'd by vernal storm,
> Lovely in death the beauteous ruin lay—
> Ye that e'er lost an angel, pity me."

His tears fell fast upon the book! He replaced it and flung himself into bed. Sleep was far from him; he closed not his eyes till the portals of light were unbarred in the east, when he fell into interrupted slumbers.

When he awoke, the morning was considerably advanced. He arose. One consolation was yet left—to see his parents happy. He went down to order his carriage; his favourite stranger, the young officer, was in waiting, and requested a private interview. They immediately retired to a separate room, when the stranger thus addressed Alonzo :

" From our short acquaintance, you may, sir, consider it singular that I should attempt to scrutinize your private concerns, and more extraordinary you may esteem it, when I inform you of my reasons for so doing Judging, however, from appearances, I have no doubt of your candour. If my questions should be deemed improper, you will tell me so."

Alonzo assured him he would treat him candidly. " This I believe, said the young officer; I take the liberty therefore to ask if you are an American ?"——"I am," answered Alonzo. " I presume, said the stranger—the question is a delicate one—I presume your family is respectable ?" " Sacredly so," replied Alonzo. " Are you married, sir ?" " I am not, and have ever been single." " Have you any prospects of connecting in marriage ?" " I have not, sir." " I may then safely proceed, said the stranger; I trust you will hear me attentively; you will judge maturely; you will decide correctly, and I am confident that you will answer me sincerely.

" A young lady of this city, with whom I am well acquainted, and to whom, indeed, I am distantly related, whose father is affluent; whose connections are eminently respectable, whose manners are engaging, whose mind is virtue, whose elegance of form and personal beauty defy competition, is the cause, sir, of this mission.—Early introduced into the higher walks of life, she has passed the rounds of fashionable company; numberless suitors sighed for her hand, whom she complaisantly dismissed without disobliging, as her heart had not yet been

touched by the tender passion of love.   Surprising as it may, however, seem, it is now
about six months since she saw in her dream
the youth who possessed the power to in-
spire her with this passion.   In her dream
she saw a young gentleman whose interesting manners and appearance, impressed her
so deeply that she found she must be unhappy without him.   She thought it was in
a mixed company she saw him, but that she
could not get an opportunity to speak to
him.   It seemed that if she could but speak
with him, all difficulties would at once be removed.   At length he approached her, and
just as she was about to address her, she awoke.

•' This extraordinary dream she had communicated to several of her acquaintance.—
Confident that she should some time or
other behold the real person whose sem-
blance she had seen in her dream, she has
never since been perfectly at ease in her
mind.   Her father, who has but two children, one beside herself, being dotingly fond
of her, has promised that if ever she meets
this unknown stranger, he will not oppose
their union, provided he is respectable, and
that, if worthy of her hand, he will make
him independent.

On my return from the inn the evening
I first saw you, I told my sister—I beg pardon, sir—I was wandering from my sub-

ject—a.ter I first met you at the inn, I fell
in company with the lady, and in a rallying
way told her that I had seen her *invisible
beau,* as we used to call the gentleman o'
the dream.   I superficially desrribed you.
person, and descanted a little on the em-
bellishments of your mind.   She listened
with some curiosity and attention; but I
had so often jested with her in this manner,
that she thought little of it.   At the play
last night, I had just been speaking to her
when I came to your box : her eyes f llow-
ed me, but no sooner had they rested on
you, than she fainted!   This was the cause
of my leaving you so abruptly, and not returning.   We conveyed her home, when
she informed me that you was the person
she had seen in her dieam !   •

   "To me only, she preferred disclosing the
circumstance at present, for reasons which
must be obvious to your understanding.—
Even her father and mother are not informed of it, and should my mission prove unsuccessful, none except you, sir, she and
myself, I hope and trust, will ever know any
thing of the matter.

   "Now, sir, it is necessary for me farther
to explain.   As singular as the circumstances which I have related may appear to
you, to me they must appear as strange. —
One valuable purpose is, however, answer-
17 *

ed thereby; it will exclude the imputation of capriciousness——the freakish whim of *love at first sight*, which exists only in novels and romances. You, sir, are young, unmarried, unaffianced, your affections free : such is the condition of the lady. She enquires not into the state of your property ! she asks not riches :—If she obtains the object of her choice, on him, as I have told you, will her father bestow affluence.—— Whatever, sir, may be your pretensions to eminence, and they may be many, the lady is not your inferior. Her education also is such as would do honour to a gentleman of taste.

"I will not extend my remarks; you perfectly understand me—what answer shall I return ?"

Alonzo sighed : for a few moments he was silent.

"Perhaps, said the stranger, you may consider the *mode* of this message as bearing the appearance of indecorum. If so, I presume, on reviewing the incidents which to—which *enforced* it, as the most safe, the *only* means of sure communication, you will change your opinion. Probably you would not wish finally to decide until you have visited the lady. This was my expectation, and I am, therefore, ready to introduce you to her presence."

"No, sir, said Alonzo, so far from considering the message indecorous, I esteem it a peculiar honour, both as respects the lady and yourself. Nor is it necessary that I should visit the lady, to confirm the truth of what you have related. You will not, sir, receive it as an adulatory compliment, when I say, that although our acquaintance is short, yet my confidence in your integrity is such as to require no corroborating facts to establish your declaration. But, sir, there are obstacles, insuperable obstacles, to the execution of the measures you would propose.

"Your frankness to me, demands, on my part, equal candour. I assured you that I was unmarried, and had no prospect of entering into matrimonial engagements; this is indeed the fact: but it is also true that my affections—my first, my earliest affections were engaged, unalienably engaged, to an object which is now no more. Perhaps you may esteem it singular; peahaps you will consider it enthusiasm; but, sir, it is impossible that my heart should admit a second and similar impression."

The stranger paused. "Recent disappointments of this nature, he replied, commonly leave the mind under such gloomy influences. Time, however, the soother of severest woes, will, though slowly, yet

surely. disperse the clouds of anguish, and
the rays of comfort and consolation will
beam upon the soul.   I wish not to be considered importunate, but the day may arrive when you may change your present determination, and then will you not regret
that you refused so advantageous an over-
ture ?"

"That day will never arrive, sir answered Alonzo : I have had time for deliberate
reflection since the melancholy event took
place.   I have experienced a sufficient
change of objects and country ; the effect
is the same. The wound is still recent,
and so it will ever remain : indeed I cannot wish it otherwise.   There is a rich and
sacred solemnity in my sorrows, sir, which
I would not exchange for the most splendid
acquirements of wealth, or the most digni-
fied titles of fame."

The young officer sat for some time silent.   "Well, sir, he said, since it is thus,
seeing that these things are so, I will urge
you no farther.   You will pardon me respecting the part I have taken in this business, since it was with the purest designs.
May consolation, comfort, and happiness,
yet be yours."

"To you and your fair friend, said Alonzo, I consider myself under the highest obligations.   The gratitude I feel I can but

feebly express. Believe me, sir, when I
tell you, (and it is all I can say,) that your
ingenuous conduct has left impressions in my
bosom which can never be obliterated "

The stranger held out his hand, which
Alonzo ardently grasped. They were silent, but their eyes spoke sympathy, and
they parted

Alonzo immediately prepared, and was
soon ready to depart. As he was stepping
into his carriage, he saw the young officer
returning. As he came up, "I must' detain
you a few moments longer, he said, and I
will give you no farther trouble. You will
recollect that the lady about whom I have
so much teazed you, when she became *acquainted* with you in her dream, believed
that if she could speak with you, all difficulties would be removed. Conscious that
this may be the case, (for with all her ac-
complishments she is a little superstitious,)
she desires to see you. You have nothing
to fear, sir; she would not for the world
yield you her hand, unless in return you
could give her your heart. Nor was she
willing you should know that she made this
request, but wished me to introduce you,
as it were by stratagem. Confident, however, that you would thus far yield to the
caprice of a lady, I chose to tell you the

truth.   She resides near by, and it will not
hinder you long."

"It is capriciousness in the extreme,"
thought Alonzo; but he told the stranger
he would accompany him—who immediately stepped into the carriage, and they
drove, by his direction, to an elegant house
in a street at a little distance, and alighted. As they entered the house, a servant
handed the stranger a note, which he hastily looked over: " Tell the gentleman I will
wait on him in a'moment," said he to the
servant, who instantly withdrew.   Turning
to Alonzo, " a person is in waiting, said he,
on urgent business; excuse me, therefore,
if it is with reluctance I retire a few moments, after I have announced you ;   I will
soon again be with you."

They then ascended a flight of stairs : the
stranger opened the door of a chamber—
"The gentleman I mentioned to you madam," he said.   Alonzo entered; the stranger closed the door and retired.   The lady
was sitting by a window at the lower end of
the room, but arose as Alonzo was announced.   She was dressed in sky-blue silk, embroidered with spangled lace ; a gemmed
tiara gathered her hair, from which was
suspended a green veil, according to the
mode of those times; a silken girdle, with
diamond clasps, surrounded her waist, and

a brilliant sparkled upon her bosom. "The stranger's description was not exaggerated. thought Alonzo; for, except one, I have never seen a more elegant figure:" and he almost wished the veil removed. that he might behold her features.

"You will please to be seated, sir, she said. I know not how—I feel an inconceivable diffidence in making an excuse for the inconveniences my silly caprices have given you."

Enchanting melody was in her voice! Alonzo knew not why, but it thrilled his bosom, electrified his soul, and vibrated every nerve of his heart. Confused and hurried sensations, melancholy, yet pleasing; transporting as the recurrence of youthful joys, enrapturing as dreams of early childhood, passed in rapid succession over his imagination!

She advanced towards him and turned aside her veil. Her eyes were suffused, and tears streamed down her cheeks.—Alonzo started—his whole frame shook—he gasped for breath!——" Melissa! he convulsively exclaimed,—God of infinite wonders, it is Melissa!"

Again will the incidents of our history produce a pause. Our sentimental readers will experience a recurrence of sympathetic sensibilities, and will attend more ea

gerly to the final scene of our drama.——.
" Melissa alive!" may they say—"impossible! Did not Alonzo see her death in the
public prints? Did not her cousin at New-
London inform him of the circumstances,
and was he not in mourning? Did not the
dying Beauman confirm the melancholy
fact? And was not the unquestionable testimony of her brother Edgar sufficient to
seal the truth of all this? Did not the sexton's wife who knew not Alonzo, corrobo-
rate it? And did not Alonzo finally read
her name, her age, and the time of her
death, on her tomb-stone, which exactly
accorded with the publication of her death
in the papers, and his own knowledge of
her age? And is not this sufficient to
prove, clearly and incontestibly prove, that
she is dead? And yet here she is again,
in all her primitive beauty and splendour!
No, this surely can never be. However
the author may succeed in his description,
in painting reanimated nature, he is no ma-
gician, or if he is, he cannot raise the
dead.

" Melissa has long since mouldered into
dust, and he has raised up some female
Martin Guerre, or Thomas Hoag——some
person, from whose near resemblance to
the deceased, he thinks to impose upon us
and upon Alonzo also, for Melissa. But it

will not do; it must be the identical Melissa herself, or it might as well be her likeness in a marble statue. What! ca/ Alonzo realize the delicacies, the tendev ness, the blandishments of Melissa in another? Can her substitute point him to the rock on New London beach, the bower on her favourite hill, or so feelingly describe the charms of nature? Can he, indeed, find in her representative those alluring graces, that pensive sweetness, those unrivalled virtues and matchless worth which he found in Melissa, and which attracted, fixed and secured the youngest affections of his soul? Impossible!———Or could the author even make it out that Alonzo was deceived by a person so nearly resembling Melissa that he could not distinguish the difference, yet to his readers he must unveil the deception, and, of course, the story will end in disappointment; it will leave an unpleasant and disagreeable impression on the mind of the reader, which in novel writing is certainly wrong. It is provec as clearly as facts can prove, that he ha\ suffered Melissa to die; and since she is dead, it is totally beyond his power to bring her to life———and so his history is intrinsically *good for nothing*.

Be not quite so hasty, my zealous censor. Did we not tell you that we were detailing facts ? Shall we disguise or discolour truth to please *your* taste ?   Have we not told you that disappointments are the lot of life? Have we not, according to the advice of the moralist, led Alonzo to the temple of philosophy, the shrine of reason, and the sanctuary of religion ? If all these fail—if in these Alonzo cannot find a balsam sufficient to heal his wounded bosom ; then if, in des pite of graves and tomb-stones, Melissa will come to his relief—will pour the balm of consolation over his anguished soul, cynical critic, can the author help it ?

It was indeed Melissa, the identical Melissa, whom Alonzo ascended a tree to catch a last glimpse of, as she walked up the avenue to the old mansion, after they had parted at the draw-bridge, on the morning of the day when she was so mysteriously removed. "Melissa !"———"Alonzo !"——— were all they could articulate : and frown not, my fair readers, if we tell you that she was instantly in his arms, while he pressed his ardent lips to her glowing cheek.

Sneer not, ye callous hearted insensibles, ye fastidious prudes, if we inform you that their tears fell in one intermingling shower, that their sighs wafted in one blended breeze.

The sudden opening of the door aroused them to a sense of their improper situa- ion ; for who but must consider it *impro-*

to find a young lady locked in the arms
of a gentleman to whom she had just been
introduced? The opening of the door,
therefore, caused them quickly to change
their *position*; not so hastily, however, but
that the young officer who then entered the
room had a glimpse of their situation.——
"Aha! said he, have I caught you? Is my
philosophic Plato so soon metamorphosed
to a *bon ton* enamarato? But a few hours
ago, sir, and you were proof against the
whole arcana of beauty, and all the artillery of the graces; but no sooner are you for
one moment *tete a tete* with a fashionable
belle, than your heroism and your resolutions are vanquished, your former ties dissolved, and your deceased charmer totally
forgotten or neglected, by the virtue of a
single glance. Well, so it is: *Amor vincit
omnia* is my motto; to thee all conquering
beauty, our firmest determinations must
bow. I cannot censure you for discovering,
though late, that one living object is really
of more intrinsic value than two dead ones.
Indeed, sir, I cannot but applaud your determination."

"The laws of honour, said Alonzo, smiling, compel me to submit to become the subject of your raillery and deception; I am
in your power."

"I acknowledge, said the officer, that I

have a little deceived you, my story was fiction founded on truth—the novel style : but for the deceptive part, you may thank your little gipsey of a nymph there, point- ng to Melissa ; she planned and I execut- ed."

"How ready you gentleman are, replied Melissa, when accused of impropriety, to cast the blame on the defenceless! So it was with our first parents, and so it is still. But you must remember that Alonzo is yet to hear my story ; there, sir, I have the ad- vantage of you."

"Then I confess, said he, looking at A- lonzo, you will be too hard for me, and so I will say no more about it."

Melissa then introduced the young officer to Alonzo, by the appellation of Capt. Wil- mot. "He is the son of my deceased un- cle, said she, a cousin to whom I am much indebted, as you shall hereafter know."

A coach drove up to the door, which Melissa informed Alonzo was her uncle's, and was sent to convey Alfred and her home. "You will have no objection to breakfast with me at my uncle's, said Alfred, if it be only to keep our cousin Melissa in counte- nance.

Alonzo did not hesitate to accept the invi- tation : They immediately therefore enter- ed the coach, a servant took care of Alon-

zo's carriage, and they drove to the seat of
Col. D——, who, with his family, received
Alonzo with much friendship and politeness. Alfred had apprized them of Alonzo's arrival in town, and of course he was
expected.

Col. D—— was about fifty years old, his
manners were majestically grave and commanding, yet polished and polite. His family consisted of an amiable wife. considerably younger than himself, and three children ; the eldest son, about ten years of age,
and two daughters, one seven, the other
four years old. Harmony and cheerfulness
reigned in his family, which diffused tranquillity and ease to its members and its
guests.

It was agreed that Alonzo should pass a
few days at the house of Melissa's uncle
when Melissa was to accompany him to
Connecticut. Alfred, with some other officers, was recruiting for the army, where
his regiment then lay, and which he was
shortly to join. He could not, therefore,
be constantly at his uncle's, though he was
principally there while Alonzo staid : but
being absent the day after his arrival, Melissa and Alonzo having retired to a room
separate from the family, she gave him the
following account of what happened after
they had parted at the old mansion.

18 *   N

" The morning after you left me, she said, John came to the bridge and called to be let in :—I immediately went to the gate, opened it, and let down the bridge. John informed me that my aunt had suddenly and unexpectedly arrived that morning in company with a strange gentleman, and that he had come for the keys, as my aunt was to visit the mansion that day. I strove to persuade John to leave the keys in my possession, and that I would make all easy with my aunt when she arrived. This, though with much reluctance, he at length consented to, and departed. Soon after this my aunt came, and without much ceremony demanded the keys, insinuating that I had obtained them from John by imposition, and for the basest purposes. This aroused me to indignation, and I answered by informing her that whatever purposes the persecutson and cruelty of my family had compelled me to adopt, my conscience, under present circumstances approved them, and I refused to give her the keys. She then ordered me to prepare to leave the mansion, and accompany her to her residence at the house of John. I told her that I had been placed there by my father, and should not consent to a removal unless by his express orders. She then left me, intimating that she would soon let me know that her authority was not to be thus trampled upon with impunity.

"I immediately raised the bridge, and made fast the gate, determining, on no con siderations, to suffer it to be opened until evening. The day passed away without any occurrence worthy of note, and as soon as it was dark, I went, opened the gate, and cautiously let down the bridge. I then returned to the mansion, and placed the candle, as we had concerted, at the window. Shortly after I heard a carriage roll over the bridge and proceed up the avenue. —My heart fluttered; I wished—I hardly knew what I did wish; but I feared I was about to act improperly, as I had no other idea but that it was you, Alonzo, who was approaching. The carriage stopped near the door of the mansion; a footstep ascended the stairs. Judge of my surprise and agitation, when my father entered the chamber! A maid and two men servants followed him. He directed me to make immediate preparations for leaving the mansion— which command, with the assistance of the servants, I obeyed with a heart too full for utterance.

"As soon as I was ready, we entered the carriage, which drove rapidly away. As we passed out of the gate, I looked back at the mansion, and saw the light of the can-

dle, which I had forgotten to remove, streaming from the window, and it was by an extraordinary effort that I prevented myself
from fainting.

" The carriage drove, as near as I could
judge, about ten miles, when we stopped at
an inn for the night, except my father, who
returned home on horseback, leaving me at
the inn in company with the servants, where
the carriage also remained. The maid was
a person who had been attached to me from
my infancy. I asked her whether she could
explain these mysterious proceedings.

" All I know, Miss, I will tell you, said
she. Your father received a letter to-day
from your aunt, which put him in a terri-
ble flutter :—he immediately ordered his
carriage and directed us to attend him. He
met your aunt at a tavern somewhere a-
way back, and she told him that the gentleman who used to come to our house so
much once, had contrived to carry you off
from the place where you lived with her;
so your father concluded to send you to
your uncle's in Carolina, and said that I
must go with you. And to tell you the
truth, Miss, I was not displeased with it ;
for your father has grown so sour of late,
that we have little peace in the house."

"By this I found that my fate was fixed,
and I gave myself up for some time to una

vailing sorrow. The maid informed me
that my mother was well, which was one
sweet consolation among my many troubles ;
but she knew nothing of my father's late
conduct.

"The next morning we proceeded, and I
was hurried on by rapid stages to the Ches-
apeak, where, with the maid and one man
servant, I was put on board a packet for
Charleston, at which place we arrived in
due time

"My uncle and his family received me
with much tenderness : the servant delivered a package of letters to my uncle from
my father. The carriage with one servant
(the driver) had returned from the Chesa-
peak to Connecticut.

"My father had but one brother and two
sisters, or which my uncle here is the youngest. One of my aunts, the old maid, who
was my *protectress* at the old mansion, you
have seen at my father's. The other was
the mother of Alfred :—she married very
young, to a gentleman in Hartford, of the
name of Wilmot, who fell before the walls
of Louisburg, in the old French war. My
aunt did not long survive him ;—her health,
which had been for some time declining,
received so serious a shock by this catastro-
phe, that she died a few months after the
melancholy tidings arrived leaving Alfred,

their only child then an infant, to the protection of his relations, who as soon as he arrived at a suitable age, placed him at school.

"My grandfather, who had the principal management of Mr. Wilmot's estate, sent my uncle, who was then young and unmarried, to Hartford, for the purpose of transacting the necessary business. Here he became acquainted with a young lady, eminent for beauty and loveliness, but without fortune, the daughter of a poor mechanic. As soon as my grandfather was informed of this attachment, he, in a very peremptory manner, ordered my uncle to break off the connection on pain of his highest displeasure. But such is the force of early impressions, (Melissa sighed) that my uncle found it impossible to submit to these firm injunctions; a clandestine marriage ensued, and my grandfather's maledictions in consequence. The union was, however, soon dissolved; my uncle's wife died in about twelve months after their marriage, and soon after the birth of the first child, which was a daughter. Inconsolable and comfortless, my uncle put the child out to nurse, and travelled to the south. After wandering about for some time, he took up his residence in Charleston, where he amassed a splendid fortune. He finally married to an amiable and respectable woman, whose ten-

derness, though it did not entirely remove,
yet greatly alleviated the pangs of .early
sorrow; and this, added to the little blan
dishments of a young family, fixed him in a
state of more contentedness than he once
ever expected to see.

"His daughter by his first wife, when
she became of pioper age, was sent to a respectable boarding-school in Boston, where
she remained until within about two years
before I came here.

" Alfred was educated at Harvard College: as soon as he had graduated, he came
here on my uncle's request, and has since
remained in his family.

"Soon after I arrived here; my uncle
came into my chamber one day " Melissa
said he, I find by your father's letters tha
he considers you to have formed an improper connection. I wish you to give me a
true statement of the matter, and if any
thing can be done to reconcile you to your
father, you may depend upon my assistance. I have seen some troubles in this
way myself, in my early days; perhaps my
counsel may be of some service."

" I immediately gave a correct account
of every particular circumstance, from the
time of my first acquaintance with you until my arrival at this house. He sat some
time silent, and then told me that my fa-

ther, he believed, had drawn the worst side of the picture ; and that he had urged him to exert every means in his power to reclaim me to obedience: That Beauman was to follow me in a few months, and that, if I still refused to yield him my hand, my father positively and solemnly declared that he would discard me forever, and strenuously enjoined it upon him to do the same. " I well know my brother's temper, continued my uncle; the case is difficult, but something must be done. I will immediately write to your father, desiring him not to proceed too rashly; in the mean time we must consider what measures to pursue. You must not, my niece, you must not be sacrificed." So saying, he left me, highly consoled that, instead of a tyrant, I had found a friend in my new protector.

" Alfred was made acquainted with the affair, and many we e the plans projected for my benefit, and abandoned as indefeasible, till an event happened which called forth all the fortitude of my uncle to support it, and operated in the end to free me from persecution.

" My uncle's daughter, by his first wife, was of a very delicate and sickly constitution, and her health evidently decreasing. After she came to this place, she was sent to a village on one of the high hills of Pe-

dee, where she remained a considerable
time, she then went to one of the inland
towns in North Carolina, from whence sne
had but just returned with Alfred when I
arrived.   Afterwards I accompanied her to
Georgetown, and other places, attended by
her father, so that she was little more
known in Charleston than myself.   But all
answered no purpose to the restoration of
her health; a confirmed hectic carried her
off in the bloom of youth.

" I was but a few months older than she;
her name was Melissa, a name which a pious grandmother had borne, and was therefore retained in the family.   Our similari-
ty of age, and in some measure of appearance, our being so little known in Charleston, and our names being the same, sugges-
ted to Alfred the idea of imposing on my
father, by passing off my cousin's death as
my own.   This would, at least, deter Beauman from prosecuting his intended journey
to Charleston; it would also give tim . for
farther deliberation, and might so operate
on my father's feelings as to soften that
obduracy of temper, which deeply disquie-
ted himself and others, and thus finally be
productive of happily effecting the designed
purpose.

" My uncle was too deeply overwhelmed
in grief to be particularly consulted on this

19

plan. He however entrusted Alfred to act
with full powers, and to use his name for
my interest, if necessary. Alfred therefore procured a publication, as of my death,
in the Connecticut papers, particularly at
New London, the native place of Beauman.   In Charleston it was generally supposed that it was the niece, and not the
daughter of Col. D——, who had died.—
This imposition was likewise practised
upon the sexton, who keeps the register of
deaths.*   Alfred then wrote a letter to my
father, in my uncle's name, stating the particulars of my cousin's death, and applying
them to me. The epitaph on her tomb-
stone was likewise so devised that it would
with equal propriety apply either to her or
to me.

"To undeceive you, Alonzo, continued
Melissa, was the next object. I consulted
with Alfred how this should be done.——
"My sister, he said, (in our private circles
he always called me by the tender name of
sister,) I am determined to see you happy
before I relinquish the business I have un-
dertaken : letters are a precarious mode of
communication ; I will make a journey to
Connecticut, find out Alonzo, visit your
friends, and see how the plan operates. I

* This was formerly the case.

am known to your father, who has ever treated me as a relative. I will return as speedily as possible, and we shall then know what measures are best next to pursue."

" I requested him to unfold the deception to my mother, and, if he found it expedient, to Vincent and Mr. Simpson, in whose friendship and fidelity I was sure he might safely confide.

" He soon departed, and returned in about two months. He found my father and mother in extreme distress on account of my supposed death : my mother's grief had brought her on the bed of sickness; but when Alfred had undeceived her she rapidly revived. My father told Alfred that he seriously regretted opposing my inclinations, and that, were it possible he could retrace the steps he had taken, he should conduct in a very different manner, as he was not only deprived of me, but Edgar also, who had gone to Holland in an official capacity, soon after receiving the tidings of my death. " I am now childless," said my father in tears. Alfred's feelings were moved, and could he then have found you, he would have told my father the truth ; but lest he should relapse from present determinations, he considered it his duty still with him, to continue the deception.

"On enquiring at your father's, at Vincent's, and at Mr Simpson's, he could learn nothing of you, except that you had gone to New London, judging possibly that you would find me there. Alfred therefore determined to proceed to that place immediately. He then confidentially unfolded to your father, Vincent, and Mr. Simpson, the scheme, desiring that if you returned you would proceed immediately to Charleston. My father was still to be kept in ignorance.

"Alfred proceeded immediately to New-London: from my cousin there he was informed of your interview with him; but from whence you then came, or where you went, he knew not; and after making the strictest enquiry, he could hear nothing more of you. By a vessel in that port, bound directly for Holland, he wrote an account of the whole affair to Edgar, mentioning his unsuccessful search to find you; and returned to Charleston.

"Alfred learnt from my friends the circumstances which occasioned my sudden removal from the old mansion. The morning you left me you was discovered by my aunt, who was passing the road in a chair with a gentleman, whom she had then but recently become acquainted with. My aunt knew you They immediately drove

to John's hut. On finding that John ha
left the keys with me, she sent him
them; and on my refusing to give them up,
she came herself, as I have before related;
and as she succeeded no better than John,
she returned and dispatched a message to
my father, informing him of the circumstances, and her suspicions of your having been
to the mansion, and that, from my having
possession of the keys and refusing to yield
them up, there was little doubt but that
we had formed a plan for my escape.

"Alarmed at this information, my father
immediately ordered his carriage, drove to
the mansion, and removed me, as I have
before informed you."

"I ought to have told you, that the maid
and man servant who attended me to
Charleston, not liking the country, and
growing sickly, were sent back by my uncle, after they had been there about two
months."

Alonzo found by this narative that John
had deceived him, when he made his enquiries of him concerning his knowledge of Melissa's removal. But this was not surprising: John was tenant to Melissa's aunt,
and subservient to all her views;—she had
undoubtedly given him instructions how to
act.

"But who was the strange gentleman
19 *

with your aunt ?" enquired Alonzo. "This I will also tell you, answered Melissa, tho' it unfolds a tale which reflects no great honour to my family.

"Hamblin was the name which this man assumed : he said he had been an eminent merchant in New York, and had left it about the time it was taken by the British. He lodged at an inn where my aunt frequently stopped when she was out collecting her rents, where he first introduced himself to her acquaintance, and ingratiated himself into her favour by art and insidiousness. He accompanied her on her visits to her tenants, and assisted her in collecting her rents. He told her, that when the war came on, he had turned his effects into money, which he had with him, and was now in pursuit of some country place where he might purchase a residence to remain during the war. To cut the story as short as possible, he finally initiated himself so far in my aunt's favour that she accepted his hand, and, contrary to my father's opinion, she married him, and he soon after persuaded her to sell her property, under pretence of removing to some populous town, and living in style. Her property, however, was no sooner sold (which my father bought for ready cash, at a low price) than he found means to realize the money, and absconded.

"It was afterwards found that his real name was Brenton; that he had left a wife and family in Virginia in indigent circumstances, where he had spent an ample fortune, left him by his father, in debauchery, and involved himself deeply in debt. He had scarcely time to get off with the booty he swindled from my aunt, when his creditors from Virginia were at his heels. He fled to the British at New York, where he rioted for a few months, was finally stabbed by a soldier in a fracas, and died the next day. He was about thirty-five years old.

"All these troubles bore so heavily upon my aunt, that she went into a decline, and died about six months ago.

"After Alfred returned from Connecticut, he wrote frequently to Vincent and Mr. Simpson, but could obtain no intelligence concerning you. It would be needless, Alonzo, to describe my conjectures, my anxieties, my feelings! The death of my cousin and aunt had kept me in crape until, at the instance of Alfred, I put it off yesterday morning at my uncle's house, which Alfred had proposed for the scene of action, after he had discovered the cause of my fainting at the theatre. I did not readily come into Alfred's plan to deceive you: "Suffer me, he said, to try the constancy of your *Leander*;——I doubt whether he would swim the Hellespont for you." This aroused my pride and confidence, and I permitted him to proceed."

Alonzo then gave Mellissa a minute account of all that happened to him from the time of their parting at the old mansion until he met with her the day before. At the mention of Beauman's fate Melissa sighed. "With how many vain fears, said she, was I perplexed, lest, by some means he should discover my existence and place of residence, after he, alas, was silent in the tomb!"

Alonzo told Melissa that he had received a letter from Edgar, after he arrived in Holland, and that he had written him an answer, just as he left Paris, informing him of his reasons for returning to America.

When the time arrived that Alonzo and Melissa were to set out for Connecticut, Melissa's uncle and Alfred accompanied them as far as Georgetown, where an affectionate parting took place: The latter returned to Charleston, and the former proceeded on their journey.

Philadelphia was now in possession of the British troops. Alonzo found Dr. Franklin's agent at Chester, transacted his business, went on, arrived at Vincent's where he left Melissa, and proceeded immediately to his father's

The friends of Alonzo and Melissa were joyfully surprised at their arrival Melissa's mother was sent for to Vincent's. Let imagination paint the meeting! As yet however they were not prepared to undecieve her father.

Alonzo found his parents in penurious circumstances; indeed, his father having the preceeding summer, been too indisposed to manage his little farm with attention, and being unable to hire labourers, his crobs had yeilded but a scanty supply, and he had been compelled to sell most of his stock to answer pressing demands. With great joy they welcomed Alonzo. whom they had given up as lost. "You still find your father poor, Alonzo, said the old gentleman, but you find him still honest.— From my inability to labour, we have latterly been a little more pressed than usual; but having now recovered my health. I trust that that difficulty will soon be removed."

Alonzo asked his father if he ever knew Dr. Franklin.

"We were school-mates, he replied and were intimately acquainted after we became young men in business for ourselves.

O

We have done each other favours; I once divided my money with Franklin on an urgent occasion to him; he afterwards repaid me with ample interest—he will never forget it."

Alonzo then related to his father all the incidents of his travels, minutely particularizing the disinterested conduct of Franklin, and then presented his father with the reversion of his estate. The old man fell on his knees, and with tears streaming down his withered cheeks, offered devout thanks to the great Dispenser of all mercies.

Alonzo then visited Melissa's father, who received him with much complacency. "I have injured, said he, my young friend, deeply injured you; but in doing this, I have inflicted a wound still deeper in my own bosom."

Alonzo desired him not to renew his sorrows. "What is past, said he, is beyond recal; but a subject of some importance to me, is the object of my present visit.—True it is, that your daughter was the object of my earliest affection—an affection which my bosom must ever retain but being separated by the will of Providence—for I view Providence as overruling all events for wise purposes—I betook myself to travel. Time, you know it is said, sir, will blunt the sharpest thorns of sorrow.—

[The old man sighed.]——In my travels I have found a lady so nearly resembling your daughter, that I was induced to sue for her hand, and have been so happy as to gain the promise of it. The favour I have to ask of you, sir, is only that you will permit the marriage ceremony to be celebrated in your house, as you know my father is poor, his house small and inconvenient, and that you will also honour me by giving the lady away. In receiving her from your hands, I shall in some measure realize former anticipations; I shall receive her in the character of Melissa."

"Ah! said Melissa's father, were it in my power—could I but give you the original; But how vain that wish! Yes, my young friend, your request shall be punctually complied with : I will take upon myself the preparations. Name your day, and if the lady is portionless, in that she shall be to me a Melissa."

Alonzo bowed his head in gratitude; and after appointing that day week, he departed.

Invitations were once more sent abroad for the wedding of Alonzo and Melissa.—Few indeed knew it to be the real Melissa, but they were generally informed of Alonzo's reason,s for preferring the celebration at her father's

The evening before the day on which the marriage was to take place, Alonzo and Melissa were sitting with the Vincents in an upper room, when a person rapped at the door below. Vincent went down, and immediately returned, introducing, to the joy and surprise of the company, Edgar!

Here, again, we shall leave it for the imagination to depict the scene of an affectionate brother, meeting a tender and only sister, whom he had long since supposed to be dead! He had been at his father's, and his mother had let him into the secret, when he immediately hastened to Vincent's. He told them that he did not stay long in Holland; that after receiving Alonzo's letter from Paris, he felt an unconquerable propensity to return, and soon sailed for America, arrived at Boston, came to New-Haven, took orders in the ministry, and had reached home that day. He informed them that Mr. Simpson and family had arrived at his father's, and some relatives whom his mother had invited.

The next morning ushered in the day in which the hero and heroine of our story were to consummate their felicity. No *cross purposes* stood ready to intervene their happiness, no obdurate father, no watchful, scowling aunt, to interrupt their transports. It was the latter end of May; nature was

arrayed in her richest ornaments, and a-
dorned with her sweetest perfumes.   The
sun blendid its mild lustre with the landscape's lovely green ; silk-winged breezes
frolicked amidst the flowers ; the spring
birds carroled in varying strains :

" The air was fragrance, and the world was love."

Evening was appointed for the ceremony, and Edgar was to be the officiating clergyman.
"To tie those bands which nought but death
can sever."
When the hour arrived, they repaired to
the house of Melissa's father, where numerous guests had assembled.   Melissa was in
troduced into the bridal apartment, and
took her seat among a brilliant circle of ladies.   She was attired in robes " white as
the southern clouds," spangled with suver,
and trimmed with deep gold lace ; her hair
hung loosely upon her shoulders, encircled
by a wreath of artificial flowers.   She had
regained all her former loveliness ; the rose
and the lily again blended their tinges in
her cheek ; again *pensive sprightliness* spark-
ed in her eye.
Alonze was now introduced, and took his
seat at the side of Melissa.   His father and
mother came next, who were placed at the
right hand of the young couple : Melissa's
20

parents followed, and were stationed at the left. Edgar then came and took his seat in front; after which the guests were summoned, who filled the room. Edgar then rising, motioned to the intended bride and bridegroom to rise also. He next turned to Alonzo's father for his sanction, who bowed assent. Then addressing his own father, with emotions that scarcely suffered him to articulate. "Do you, sir, said he, give this lady to that gentleman?" A solemn silence prevailed in the room. Melissa was extremely agitated, as her father, slowly rising, and with down-cast eyes,

"Where tides of heavy sorrow swell'd,"

took her trembling hand, and conveying it into Alonzo's, "May the smiles of heaven rest upon you, he said; may future blessings crown your present happy prospects; and may your latter days never be embittered by the premature loss of near and dear————"

Pungent grief here choaked his utterance, and at this moment Melissa, falling upon her knees, "Dear father! she exclaimed, bursting into tears, pardon deception; acknowledge your daughter—your own Melissa!"

Her father started—he gazed at her with scrutinizing attention, and sunk back in his chair.—" My daughter ! he cried—God of mysterious mercy ! it is my daughter !"

The guests caught the contagious sympathy ; convulsive sobs arose from all parts of the room. Melissa's father clasped her in his arms—"And I receive thee as from the dead ' he said. I am anxious to hear the mighty mystery unfolded. But first let the solemn rites for which we are assembled be concluded ; let not an old man's anxiety interrupt the ceremony."

" But you are apprised, sir, said Alonzo, of my inability to support your daughter according to her deserts."

" Leave that to me, my young friend, replied her father. I have enough : my children are restored, and I am happy."

Melissa soon resumed her former station. The indissoluble knot was tied : they sat down to the wedding feast, and mirth and hilarity danced in cheerful circles.

Before the company retired, Edgar related the most prominent incidents of Alonzo and Melissa's history, since they had been absent. The guests listened with attention : they applauded the conduct of our new bride and bridegroom, in which Melissa's father cordially joined. They rejoiced to find that Alonzo's father had regained his fortune, and copious libations were

poured forth in honour of the immortal
Franklin.

And now, reader of sensibility, indulge
the pleasing sensations of thy bosom—for
Alonzo and Melissa are MARRIED.

Alonzo's father was soon in complete re-
possession of his former property.   The
premises from which he had been driven
by his unfeeling creditors, were yielded up
without difficulty, and to which he immediately removed.   He not only recovered
the principal of the fortune he had lost,
but the damages and the interest ; so that,
although like Job, he had seen affliction,
like him his latter days were better than
his beginning.   But wearied with the bus
tles of life, he did not again enter into the
mercantile business, but placing his money
at interest in safe hands, lived retired on
his little farm.

A few days after the wedding, as Melissa was sitting with Alonzo, Edgar and her
parents, she asked her father whether the
old mansion was inhabited.

"Not by human beings, he replied.——
Since it has fallen into my hands I have
leased it to three or four different families,
who all left it under the foolish pretence or
impression of hearing noises and seeing
frightful objects, and such is the supersti-
tion of the people that no one now, will

ven.ure to try it again, though I suppose
its inhabitants to consist only of rats and
mice."

Melissa then informed them of all that
had happened when she was there, the alarming noises and horrible appearances she
had been witness to, and in which she was
confident her senses had not deceived her.
Exceedingly astonished at her relation; it
was agreed that Edgar and Alonzo, properly attended, should proceed to the mansion,
in order to find whether any discoveries
could Le made which might tend to the
elucidation of so mysterious an affair.

For this purpose they chose twenty men,
armed them with muskets and swords, and
proceeded to the place, where they arrived
in the dusk of the evening, having chosen
'that season as the most favourable to their
designs.

They found the drawbridge up, and the
gate locked, as Edgar's father said he had
left them. They entered and secured them
in the same manner. When they came to
the house, they cautiously unlocked the
door, and proceeded to the chamber, where
they struck a fire and lighted candles, which
they had brought with them. It was then
agreed to plant fifteen of the men at suitable distances around the mansion, and re-

tain five in the chamber with Alonzo and
Edgar.

The men, who were placed around the
house, were stationed behind trees, stumps
or rocks, and where no object presented,
lay flat on the ground, with orders not to
stir, or discover themselves, let what would
ensue, unless some alarm should be given
from the house.

Alonzo and Edgar were armed with pis-
tols and side arms, and posted themselves
with the five men in the chamber, taking
care that the lights should not shine against
the window shutters, so that nothing could
be discovered from without.   Things thus
arranged, they observed almost an implicit
silence, no one being allowed to speak, except in a low whisper.

For a long time no sound was heard except the hollow roar of winds in the neighbouring forest, their whistling around the
angles of the mansion, or the hoarse mur-
mers of the distant surge.   The night was
dark, and only illuminated by the feeble
twinkling of half clouded stars.

They had watched until about midnight,
when they were alarmed by noises in the
rooms below, among which they could distinguish footsteps and human voices. A-
lonzo and Edgar, then taking each a pistol
in one hand, and a drawn sword in the oth-

er, ordered their men to follow them, prepared for action. Coming to the head of the stairs, they saw a brilliant light streaming into the hall; they therefore concluded to take no candles, and to prevent discovery they took off their shoes. When they came into the hall opposite the door of the room from whence the light and noises proceeded, they discovered ten men genteelly dressed, sitting around a table, on which was placed a considerable quantity of gold and silver coin, a number of glasses and several decanters of wine. Alonzo and his party stood a few minutes, listening to the following discourse, which took place among this *ghostly* gentry.

"Well, boys, we have made a fine haul this trip."——"Yes, but poor Bob, though, was plump'd over by the d——d skulkers!' —"Aye, and had we not tugged bravely at the oars, they would have hook'd us."—— "Rascally cow-boys detained us too long." ——"Well, never mind it; let us knock around the wine, and then divide the spoil."

At this moment, Alonzo and Edgar, followed by the five men, rushed into the room, crying. "*Surrender, or you are all dead men!*" In an instant the room was involved in pitchy darkness; a loud crash was heard, then a scampering about the floor, and a noise as if several doors shut

to, with violence.   They however gave the
alarm to the men without, by loudly shout-
ing *"Look out;"* and immediately the discharge of several guns was heard around the
mansion.   One of the men flew up stairs
and brought a light; but, to their utter a-
mazement, no person was to be discovered
in the room except their own party.   The
table, with its apparatus, and the chairs on
which these now invisible beings had sat,
had disappeared, not a single trace of them
being left.

While they stood petrified with aston-
ishment, the men from without called for
admittance.   The door being unlocked,
they led in a stranger wounded, whom they
immediately discovered to be one of those
they had seen at the table.

The men who had been stationed around
the mansion informed, that some time before the alarm was made, they saw a number of persons crossing the yard from the
western part of the enclosure, towards the
house; that immediately after the shout
was given, they discovered several people
running back in the same direction: they
hailed them, which being disregarded, they
fired upon them, one of whom they brought
down, which was the wounded man they
had brought in.   The others, though they
pursued them got off.

The prisoner's wound was not dangerous, the ball had shattered his arm, and glanced upon his breast. They dressed his wound as well as they could, and then requested him to unfold the circumstances of the suspicious appearance in which he was involved.

"First promise me, on your honour, said the stranger, that you will use your influence to prevent my being punished or imprisoned."

This they readily agreed to, on condition that he would conceal nothing from them—and he gave them the following relation:

That they were a part of a gang of *illicit traders;* men who had combined for the purpose of carrying on a secret and illegal commerce with the British army on Long Island, whom, contrary to the existing laws, they supplied with provisions, and brought off English goods, which they sold at very extortionate prices. But this was not all; they also brought over large quantities of counterfeit continental money, which they put off among the American's for live stock, poultry, produce, &c. which they carried to the Island. The counterfeit money they purchased by merely paying for the printing; the British having obtained copies of the American emission, struck im-

mense quantities of it in New-York, and
insidiously sent it out into the country, in
order to sink our currency.

This gang was likewise connected with
the. cow-boys, who made it their business
to steal, not only milch cows, and other
cattle, but also hogs and sheep, which they
drove by night to some convenient place
on the shores of the Sound, where these
thief-partners received them, and conveyed
them to the British.

"In our excursions across the Sound,
continued the wounded man, we had frequently observed this mansion, which, from
every appearance, we were convinced was
uninhabited :—we therefore selected it as a
suitable place for our future rendezvous,
which had therefore been only in the open
woods. To cross the moat we dragged up
an old canoe from the sea shore, which we
concealed in the bushes as soon as we re-
crossed from the old mansion. To get over
the wall we used ladders of ropes, placing
a flat of thick board on the top of the spike
driven into the wall. We found more difficulty in getting into the house :—we
however at length succeeded, by tearing
away a part of the back wall, where we fitted in a door so exactly, and so nicely
painted it, that it could not be distinguished from the wall itself. This door was so

constructed, that on touching a spring, it would fly open, and when unrestrained, would shut to with violence. Finding the apartment so eligibie for our purpose, and fearing that at some future time we might be disturbed either by the owner of the building or some tenant, we cut similar doors into every room of the house, so that on an emergency we could traverse every apartment without access to the known doors. Trap-doors on a similar construction, communicated with the cellar:—the table, which you saw us sitting around, stood on one of those, which, on your abrupt appearance, as soon as the candles were extinguished, was with its contents, precipitated below, and we made our escape by those secret doors, judging, that although you had seen us, if we could get off, you would be unabie to find out any thing which might lead to cur discovery.

"A circumstance soon occurred, which tended to embarrass our plans, and at first seemed to menace their overthrow. Our assembling at the mansion was irregular, as occasion and circumstances required; often not more than once a week, but sometimes more frequent, and always in the night.— Late one night, as we were proceeding to the mansion, and had arrived near it, suddenly one of the chamber windows was o pened, and a light issued from within. We entered the house with caution, and soon discovered that some person was in the chamber from whence we had seen the light. We remained until all was silent, and then entered the chamber by one of our secret doors, and to our inexpressible surprise, beheld a beautiful young lady a-sleep on the only bed in the room. We cautiously retired, and reconnoitering all parts of the mansion, found that she was the only inhabitant except ourselves. The singularity of her being there alone, is a circumstance we have never been able to discover, but it gave us fair hopes of easily procuring her ejectment. We then immediately withdrew, and made preparations to dispossess the fair tenant of the premises to which we considered ourselves more properly entitled, as possessing a prior incumbency.

"We did not effect the completion of our apparatus under three or four days. As soon as we were prepared, we returned to the mansion. As we approached the house, it appears the lady heard us, for again she suddenly flung up a window and held out a candle : we skulked from the light, but feared she had a glimpse of us.—After we had got into the house we were still until we

supposed her to be asleep, which we found
to be the case on going to her chamber.

"We then stationed one near her bed,
who, by a loud rap on the floor with a cane,
appeared to arouse her in a fright.   Loud
noises were then made below, and some of
them ran heavily up the stairs which led to
her chamber; the person stationed in the
room whispering near her bed—she raised
herself up, and he fled behind the curtains.
Soon after she again lay down; he approached nearer the bed with a design to lay his
hand, on which he had drawn a thin sheet-
lead glove, across her face; but discovering her arm on the out side of the bed-
clothes, he grasped it—she screamed and
sprang up in the bed; the man then left
the room.

"As it was not our intention to injure
the lady, but only to drive her from the
house, we concluded we had sufficiently
alarmed her, and having extinguished the
lights, were about to depart, when we heard
her descending the stairs.   She came down
and examined the doors, when one of our
party, in a loud whisper, crying "*away!
away;*" she darted up stairs, and we left
the house.

"We did not return the next night, in
order to give her time to get off; but the
night after we again repaired to the man

sion, expecting that she had gone, but we
were disappointed. As it was late when we
arrived, she was wrapped in sleep, and we
found that more forcible measures must be
resorted to before we could remove her, and
for such measures we were amply prepared.

The stranger then unfolded the mysteries
of that awful night, when Melissa was so
terrified by horrible appearances. One of
the tallest and most robust of the gang, was
attired, as has been described, when he appeared by her bed side. The white robe
was an old sheet, stained in some parts with
a liquid red mixture; the wound in his
breast was artificial, and the blood issuing
therefrom was only some of this mixture,
pressed from a small bladder, concealed under his robe. On his head and face he wore
a mask, with glass eyes——the mask was
painted to suit their purposes. The bloody
dagger was of wood, and painted.

Thus accoutred, he took his stand near
Melissa's bed, having first blown out the
candles she had left burning, and discharged a small pistol. Perceiving this had a-
wakened her, a train of powder was fired
in the adjoining room opposite the secret
door, which was left open, in order that
the flash might illuminate her apartment;
then several large cannon balls were rolled
through the rooms over her head, imitative

of thunder.   The person in her room then
uttered a horrible groan, and gliding along
by her bed, took his stand behind the curtains, near the foot.   The noises below, the
cry of murder, the firing of the second pistol, and the running up stairs, were all cor-
responding scenes to impress terror on her
imagination.   The pretended ghost then
advanced in front of her bed, while lights
were slowly introduced, which first shone
faintly, until they were ushered into the
room by the private door, exhibiting the
person before her in all his horrific appearances.   On her shrieking, and shrinking into the bed, the lights were suddenly extinguished, and the person, after commanding
her to be gone in a hoarse voice, passed a-
gain to the foot of the bed, shook it violently, and made a seeming attempt to get upon it, when, perceiving her to be springing
up, he fled out of the room by the secret
door, cautiously shut it, and joined his com-
panions.

   The operators had not yet completed
their farce, or rather, to Melissa, tragedy.
They had framed an image of paste-board,
in human shape, arrayed it in black, its
eyes being formed of large pieces of what
is vulgarly called *fox-fire,** made into the

---

* A sort of decayed or rotten wood, which in the night looks
like coals of fire, of a bright whitish colour. It emits a faint
light.

likeness of human eyes, some material be
ing placed in its mouth, around which was
a piece of the thinest scarlet tiffany, in
order to make it appear of a flame colour
They had also constructed a large combustible ball, of several thicknesses of paste-
board, to which a match was placed. The
image was to be conveyed into her room,
and placed, in the dark, before her bed;--
while in that position, the ball was to be
rubbed over with phosphorus, the match
set on fire, and rolled across her chamber,
and when it burst, the image was to vanish,
by being suddenly conveyed out of the private door, which was to close the scene for
that night. But as Melissa had now arisen
and lighted candles, the plan was defeated.

While they were consulting how to pro-
cee l, they heard her unlock her chamber
dce , and slowly descend the stairs. Fearing a discovery, they retired with their
lights, and the person who had been in her
chamber, not having yet stripped off his
ghostly habiliments, laid himself down on
one side of the hall. The man who had the
image, crowded himself with it under the
stairs she was descending. On her dropping the candle, when she turned to flee to
her chamber, from the sight of the same object which had appeared at her bed-side,
the person under the stairs presented the

image at their foot, and at the same instan
the combustible ball was prepared, and rolled through the hall; and when on its bursting she fainted, they began to grow alarmed;
but on finding that she recovered and regained her chamber, they departed, for
that time, from the house.

"Our scheme, continued the wounded
man, had the desired effect. On returning
a few evenings after, we found the lady
gone and the furniture removed. Several
attempts were afterwards made to occupy
the house, but we always succeeded in soon
frightening the inhabitants away."

Edgar and Alonzo then requested their
prisoner to show them the springs of the
secret doors, and how they were opened.
The springs were sunk in the wood, which
being touched by entering a gimblet hole
with a piece of pointed steel, which each
of the gang always had about him, the door
would fly open, and fasten again in shutting
to. On opening the trap-door over which
the gang had sat when they first discovered
them, they found the table and chairs, with
the decanters broken, and the money, which
they secured. In one part of the cellar they
were shown a kind of cave, its mouth covered with boards and earth—here the company
kept their furniture, and to this place would
they have removed it, had they not been so

suddenly frightened away. The canoe they found secreted in the bushes beyond the canal.

It was then agreed that the man should go before the proper authorities in a neighbouring town, and there, as state's evidence, make affidavit of what he had recited, and as complete a developement of the characters concerned i· the business as possible, when he was to be released. The man enquired to what town they were to go which, when they had informed him, " Then, said he, it will be in my power to perform one deed of justice before I leave the country, as leave it I must, immediately after I have given in my testimony, or I shall be assassinated by scme of those who will be implicated in the transaction I have related."

He then informed them, that while he, with the gang, was prosecuting the illicit trade, a British ship came and anchored in the Sound, which they supplied with provisions, but that having at one time a considerable quantity on hand, the ship sent its boat on shore, with an officer and five men, to fetch it; the officer came with them on shore, leaving the men in the boat: " As we were about to carry the provisions on board the boat, continued the man, a party of Americans fired upon us, and

wounded the officer in the thigh, who fell:
" I shall be made prisoner, said he, taking
out his purse; keep this, and if I live and
regain my liberty, perhaps you may have
an opportunity of restoring it:—alarm the
boat's crew, and shift for yourselves." The
boat was alarmed, returned to the ship, and
we saved ourselves by flight.

" This happened about four months ago:
the ship soon after sailed for New York,
and the officer was imprisoned in the gaol
of the town to which we are to go; I can
therefore restore him his purse."

The man farther informed them, that
they had several times come near being taken, and the last trip they were fired upon,
and one of their party killed.

" They immediately set out for the afore-
said town, after having dismissed their fifteen men; and when they arrived there,
Alonzo and Edgar accompanied their prisoner to the gaol. On making the proper
enquiries, they were conducted into a dark
and dirty apartment of the gaol, where
were several prisoners in irons. The British officer was soon distinguished among
them by his regimentals. Though enveloped in filth and dust, his countenance appeared familiar to Alonzo; and on a few
moments recollection, he recognized in the
manacled officer, the generous midshipman.

Jack Brown, who had so disinterestedly re-
lieved him, when he escaped from the prison in London!

In the fervency of his feelings, Alonzo
flew to him and clasped him in his arms.
" What do I behold! he cried. My friend,
my brave deliverer, in chains in my own
country !"

" The fortune of war, boy! said Jack—
it might have been worse. But my lad, I
am heartily glad to see you; how has it
fared with you since you left Old England?"
—" We will talk of that by and by," said
Alonzo.

There were then some American officers
of distinction in town, with whom Edgar
was acquainted, to whom he applied for the
relief of the noble sailor :——and as there
were several other British prisoners in gaol
it was agreed that a cartel should be immediately sent to New York to exchange them.
Alonzo had, therefore, the satisfaction to see
the irons knocked off of his liberal hearted
benefactor, and his prison doors opened.

The man they had taken at the mansion,
returned him his purse, containing only
twenty-five guineas, of which Jack gave
him ten. " There, boy, said he, you have
been honest, so I will divide with you."

They then repaired to an inn. Jack,
whose wound was healed, was put under

the hands of a barber, cleaned, furnished
with a change of clothes, and soon appeared in a new attitude.

He informed Alonzo, that soon after he
left England, his ship was ordered for A-
merica : that the price of provisions growing high, it had taken almost all his wages
to support his family ; that he had sent
home his last remittance just before he was
taken, reserving only the twenty-five guineas which had been restored him that day.
—"But I have never despaired, said he;
the great Commodore of life orders all for
the best. My tour of duty is to serve my
king and country, and provide for my dear
Poll and her chicks, which, if I faithfully
perform, I shall gain the applause of the
Commander."

When the cartel was ready to depart,
Alonzo, taking Jack apart from the company, presented him with a draught of five
hundred pounds sterling, on a merchant in
New York, who privately transacted business with the Americans. " Take this, my
friend, said he ; you can ensure it by con-
verting it into bills of exchange on London.
Though you once saw me naked, I can now
conveniently spare this sum, and it may
assist you in buffeting the billows of life."—
The generous tar shed tears of gratitude,
and Alonzo enjoyed the pleasure of seeing

him depart, calling down blessings on the head of his reciprocal benefactor.

The man who came with Alonzo and Edgar from the mansion, then went before the magistrates of the town, and gave his testimony and affidavit, by which it appeared that several eminent characters of Connecticut were concerned in this illicit trade. They then released him, gave him the money they had found in the cellar at the mansion, and he immediately left the town. Precepts were soon after issued for a number of those traders; several were taken, among whom were some of the gang, and others who were only concerned—but most of them absconded, so that the company and their plans were broken up.

When Alonzo and Edgar returned home and related their adventure, they were all surprised at the fortitude of Melissa in being enabled to support her spirits in a solitary mansion, amidst such great, and so many terrors.

It was now that Alonzo turned his attention to future prospects. It was time to select a place for domestic residence. He consulted Melissa, and she expressively mentioned the little secluded village, where

" Ere fate and fortune frown'd severe,

hey projected scenes of connubial bliss, and

planned the structure of their family edifice. This intimation accorded with the ardent wishes of Alonzo. The site formerly marked out, with an adjoining farm, was immediately purchased, and suitable buildings erected, to which Alonzo and Melissa removed the ensuing summer.

The clergyman of the village having recently died in a *good old age*, Edgar was called to the pastoral charge of this unsophisticated people. Here did Melissa and Alonzo repose after the storms of adversity were past. Here did they realize all the happiness which the sublunary hand of time apportions to mortals. The varying seasons diversified their joys, except when Alonzo was called with the militia of his country, wherein he bore an eminent commission, to oppose the enemy; and this was not unfrequent, as in his country's defence he took a very conspicuous part. Then would anxiety, incertitude, and disconsolation possess the bosom of Melissa, until dissipated by his safe return. But the happy termination of the war soon removed all cause of these disquietudes.

Soon after the close of the war, Alonzo received a letter from his friend, Jack Brown, dated at an interior parish in England,—in which, after pouring forth abundance of gratitude, he informed, that on returning to England he procured his discharge from the navy, sold his house, and removed into the country, where he had set up an inn with the sign of *The Grateful American.* "You have made us all happy, said he; my dear Poll blubbered like a fresh water sailor in a hurricane, when I told her of your goodness. My wife, my children, all hands upon deck are yours. We have a good run of business, and are now under full sail, for the land of prosperity."

Edgar married to one of the Miss Simpsons, whose father's seat was in the vicinity of the village. The parents of Alonzo and Melissa were their frequent visitors, as were also Vincent and his lady, with many others of their acquaintance, who all rejoiced in their happy situation, after such a diversity of troubles. Alfred was generally once a year their guest, until at length he married and settled in the mercantile business in Charleston, South Carolina.

To our hero and heroine, the rural charms of their secluded village were a source of ever pleasing variety. Spring, with its verdurous fields, flowery meads, and vocal groves ; its vernal gales, purling rills, and its evening whippoorwill: summer, with its embowering shades, reflected in the glassy lake, and the long, pensive, yet sprightly notes of the solitary strawberry-bird :* its lightning and its thunder ; autumn with its mellow fruit, its yellow foliage and decaying verdure ; winter with its hoarse, rough blasts, its icy beard and snowy mantle, all tended to thrill with sensations of pleasing transi tion, the feeling bosoms of *Alonzo and Melissa.*

---

* A bird which, in the New England states, makes its first appearance about the time strawberries begin to ripen. Its song is lengthy, and consists of a variety of notes, commencing sprightly, but ending plaintive and melancholy.

THE END

www.ingramcontent.com/pod-product-compliance
Lightning Source LLC
Chambersburg PA
CBHW030807020726
47499CB00006B/1798